PYRATES #3

DEAD MAN'S CHEST

CHRIS ARCHER

SCHOLASTIC INC.
New York Toronto London Auckland Sydney
Mexico City New Delhi Hong Kong Buenos Aires

ISBN 0-439-36853-7

Copyright © 2003 17th Street Productions,
an Alloy, Inc. company
All rights reserved.
Published by Scholastic Inc.

Produced by 17th Street Productions,
an Alloy, Inc. company
151 West 26th Street
New York, NY 10001

12 11 10 9 8 7 6 5 4 3 2   3 4 5 6 7 8/0

Printed in the U.S.A.   40
First printing, March 2003

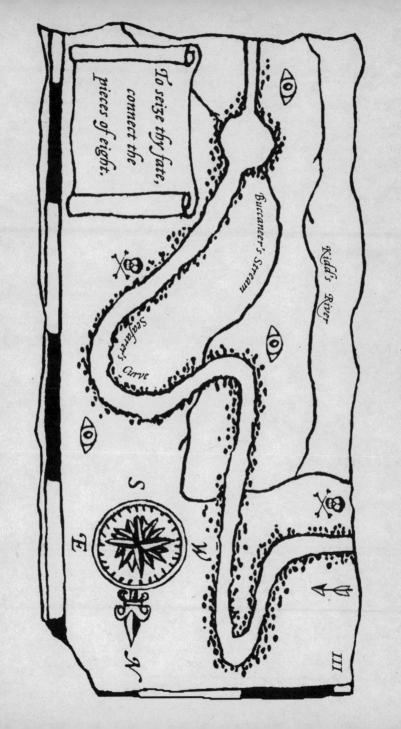

To seize thy fate, connect the pieces of eight.

Buccaneer's Stream

Kidd's River

Seafarer's Curve

III

One

IN THE DARK

George van Gelder pulled the covers up to his chin and tried not to scream.

It was quiet, or at least as quiet as it got inside the van Gelder house in the middle of downtown New York City. Normal sounds intruded from outside: car horns, dogs barking, the occasional siren. George was used to those sounds. George was also used to the creaks and groans that their house usually made. The house was over three hundred years old, and old houses made creepy noises. George knew that.

But tonight was different. Earlier in the day he and his friend Shannon had narrowly escaped after being kidnapped. Their captor, a man named Roulain, lived down the street and was still at large. Which was why George was lying in bed, terrified, eyes wide open, teeth chattering, heart pounding.

George had always liked the fact that he lived in a house built by the notorious pirate Captain Kidd. But tonight it didn't seem so cool to live in an old house that made old-house noises. Most nights George fell asleep as soon as his head hit the pillow. But tonight every time he was about to drift off, he heard a—

Groannnn.

There it was again.

George had heard similar sounds every night. But now, in the dark, he couldn't help being afraid. He pictured Roulain and his men emerging from the trapdoor in the basement. Quietly opening the basement door. Creeping stealthily up the stairs. Stopping outside George's room. Turning the handle—

Thump!

"Aaah!"

George sat bolt upright in bed. A dark and menacing shadow danced against the wall of his room, and George cowered, his eyes shut tight, waiting for the worst.

But nothing happened.

After a few seconds George opened his eyes very slowly. Pale moonlight spilled through his window, and George immediately saw what had cast the shadow. It was a stray cat on the windowsill that had probably just jumped from the fire escape of the building next door. It looked quizzically through the window at George as if to ask, "What, are you scared of *me*?"

"George?"

Peter van Gelder stood in George's doorway, his eyes sleepy but concerned. "Is everything all right?" George's dad was a college professor who taught history. Usually his thinning hair was neatly combed, but now it stood up in at least three different directions. He had obviously been fast asleep before George had screamed.

"Yeah, Dad. I'm . . . fine. I just had a bad dream, that's all."

George's dad looked down at the book beside George's bed. *Cutthroat Pirates of the South Seas*. He had given it to George for his birthday two weeks earlier.

"Maybe you should think twice about your bedtime reading." But Peter van Gelder was smiling, not mad. "That book will fill your head with all sorts of scary ideas."

"Um, yeah. I guess. Sorry."

His father looked at him like he wanted to say something, then just shook his head.

"No problem. Just remember, there aren't any real pirates. Not anymore."

"Yeah, right, Dad. Thanks."

"Sure. Have a good night, George."

" 'Night, Dad."

George's dad closed the door with a soft click,

and George heard his footsteps tread softly back to his room.

George felt a pang of guilt. He had been keeping a pretty big secret from his dad, and the kidnapping was only a part of it. He couldn't tell his dad why he had really screamed just then, why he was so afraid to be in their house tonight. That was a secret he shared with three of his friends from school: Derrick, Shannon, and Renee. The secret belonged to all of them, and it wouldn't be right for him to confess it on his own.

And what a secret it was! The four of them had discovered a map in the attic that had been left behind by Captain Kidd himself. They'd followed the map to a trapdoor in George's basement, a trapdoor that led to a series of tunnels under the city. With the help of a homeless boy named Paul who lived in the tunnels, George and his friends were trying to find Captain Kidd's hidden treasure—a priceless diamond called the Eye of Eternity.

The only problem was that Roulain (who went by the name "Leroy" underground to protect his identity) wanted the Eye, too. He had a whole criminal gang working for him, and the thugs would hurt anyone who got in their way. They'd kidnapped Shannon and George, but thanks to Renee's rock-climbing skills, they'd been able to escape. They were free, but so was Roulain. He was dangerous, and he knew the kids were on to him. Even worse, he lived on George's block, and until today George had thought he was just a nice, normal neighbor. How long would it be before he tried something else against them?

The kids had kept their quest a secret up till now. They knew their parents would never let them explore the tunnels, looking for treasure. It had been fun and exciting, living a real-life pirate adventure. But now George wondered if things had gotten too dangerous. Maybe they should tell their parents what was going on, or even the police.

It wasn't a secret George could tell on his own, but maybe he could convince the others that it was the best thing to do. "I'm sure going to suggest it tomorrow," George whispered to himself, pulling the covers up closer to his face.

Creaakk.

No real pirates, his dad had said. Not anymore. If he only knew.

"George! You look *terrible!*" Derrick exclaimed when he saw George in the lunchroom the next morning. Derrick was George's best friend, so if he thought George looked bad, then it must be true.

George winced. It was the third time that morning someone had mentioned how tired he looked.

His eyelids felt like they had five-ton weights taped to them, and his entire body felt like he was moving through a sea of molasses. He wanted nothing more than to curl up in his bed and sleep for about twenty hours straight.

"I didn't sleep very well last night," George replied.

"I don't blame you!" Derrick said. Derrick's own black hair looked mussed, and only half of his short-sleeved jersey was tucked into his jeans. He looked like he might not have slept so well himself. "I still can't believe what happened to you and Shannon. I mean, it's just so . . . so . . ."

"It's unreal is what it is," Renee chimed in. She pushed a few long strands of her golden-blond hair behind her ear as she spoke. She looked concerned. "This whole pirate adventure has become so much more dangerous than I ever thought it would." She jammed both of her hands into the pockets of her khakis in frustration.

"Hey." George turned back to Derrick, suddenly remembering something. "Did you try getting into that handheld computer again?"

Derrick nodded, seeming to wake up a little. "Oh, yeah. I used 'Roulain' as the password this time, and I guess it worked."

"You *guess*?" George asked. About a week before Shannon and George had been kidnapped by Roulain, they'd found a handheld computer in the tunnels that they believed belonged to Leroy. At the time they hadn't realized that Roulain and Leroy were one and the same. The computer was protected by some kind of password program, and Derrick had been going crazy trying to think of words Leroy might use. "What do you mean? Are there any clues in there?"

Derrick scrunched up his face. "Well, I found a bunch of names and addresses, probably the guys who work for Roulain. And there *is* a daybook in there. The only problem is I think it's in code."

George looked over at Renee and Shannon to get their reactions, but it seemed like they weren't even paying attention. "What do you mean?"

Derrick sighed. "Like on a certain day it'll have three letters—STJ or JRF. It must mean something, but who knows what? And who knows if it even has anything to do with the treasure?"

George frowned. They'd finally gotten into the computer, but it appeared to be yet another dead end. He looked at his friends. Derrick and Renee both seemed really worried—still freaked out by the kidnapping, most likely. George glanced over at Shannon, who was sitting off a bit from the others. She was nervously twirling a finger through her dark brown hair, which she usually highlighted with some kind of bright, outrageous color. But today she had just left it plain. She stopped playing with her hair suddenly, as if she'd just realized she'd been doing it. But after a few moments she started toying with the necklace she wore instead.

He couldn't tell how Shannon felt. Her face was a total blank. But the fact that she was quiet said a lot, actually. Shannon was never quiet. She must be as frightened to the bone as he had been last night. After all, it was the two of them who had been held captive in Roulain's apartment, not knowing what horrible plans he had for them. . . .

"Well . . ." George started, but his voice trailed off. He knew what had to be said but was actually reluctant to say it. He didn't want to be the one to suggest giving up on something he'd dreamed of all his life.

But before he could continue, Derrick interrupted him. "George, we have something to tell you."

George's three friends looked at one another, but none of them seemed to want to go first. None of them could even look George in the eye.

George had a sinking feeling in his stomach.

"You see, George," Renee began. "We think this whole thing has gotten kind of out of control."

George looked around and saw Derrick and Shannon nodding in agreement.

"When we started all of this, it was for fun. Well . . . and for money, too, I guess."

Renee stopped, looking at the others. Derrick continued in her place: "But now that we know what we're up against, we think it's just too much. We're just a bunch of kids, but Roulain and his men, well, they're . . . they're *really dangerous*. We think . . ."

"We think we should quit before something more serious happens," Renee said. "Because these guys really mean business, and they're up to no good, and . . . well . . . we're out of our league."

George looked around the group, looking each of his friends in the face.

Shannon sat still as stone. Finally, she nodded slowly, like it made her sad to do so. "I agree."

George swallowed, his throat tight. He couldn't believe it. He had come here ready to tell them all the same thing they had just told him. That things were getting too dangerous. That they were in over their heads. That they should think about quitting.

So why did he suddenly feel like that would be a big mistake?

"I can't believe this, guys. I mean, I know things have gotten kind of weird, but are we going to just quit at the first sign of trouble?"

Derrick, Renee, and Shannon all looked at him like they couldn't believe he was saying it. *George* couldn't believe he was saying it. Where were these words coming from?

"We took an oath, and we agreed to go after this treasure. And I think we should keep going until we find it."

"You don't think we should call the police?" Renee looked dumbfounded.

"If we go to the cops, what are we going to say?"

"That Roulain kidnapped you, of course!"

"But we don't have any proof!" George said. "It's our word against his. He's an adult, and we're just a bunch of kids."

"But we can show them the tunnels, show them how the elevator goes up to Roulain's apartment," Renee said, looking at George like he was crazy.

"I don't think that's a good idea, Renee. Roulain will say he didn't kidnap us—we were trespassing in his apartment! If anything, *we'll* be the ones getting in trouble while Roulain is free to search for the Eye of Eternity and take his time!"

They all sat there in silence, letting George's words sink in. George could see that his words were starting to make sense to them.

"But George, aren't you afraid?" asked Derrick finally. "I mean, how hard would it be for Roulain to get into your house through the tunnel in your basement?"

George hesitated.

All at once he felt the tiredness of having

stayed up half the night come crashing down on him. George opened his mouth, about to argue with Derrick. But wasn't Derrick right? What answer could he possibly make?

Then it hit him.

"There's no reason to be afraid! That tunnel goes forty feet straight up! We need to tie a rope to something in the basement just to get up and down ourselves. Unless Roulain's grown since the last time I saw him, he's going to have trouble getting into my basement that way!"

"I don't know," said Shannon, poking at her sandwich. "Roulain's got a lot of tools and gizmos down there. Maybe he's got an extension ladder that he could use to get up."

"Well, then we can just cover the trapdoor with something heavy when we're not using it," George retorted. "Like books—there are a ton of them in my basement. If we pile enough on, there's no way Roulain could get past the trapdoor. You know how heavy those books are." Each of them had complained about having to move the heavy boxes of books that George's dad kept in the basement. They were heavy, all right. Still, the group didn't look convinced.

"Or," he continued, "we could add an extra latch to the door, with a lock. I helped my dad put one on my grandma's back door. It's really easy, and it's strong."

George sat back and looked at the others as they exchanged glances. It looked like they were softening. He might actually pull this off!

"Okay . . ." said Renee, still skeptical. "But what about when we're in the tunnels? What if they come along and see our rope, just hanging there waiting to be found?"

George hesitated. He hadn't thought about that.

"That's not so hard," Derrick said. George looked at him in surprise. Derrick was arguing *his* side? "We can rig up a way of hiding it. We can set it up so that you can't see the rope unless you know it's there. You know, camouflage. I have a couple of ideas I'll draw up."

Renee didn't look convinced. "But what about when we use the tunnel to go down? What if they're waiting for us? They could ambush us the second we got down there!"

"We could use my web cam." George couldn't believe it. Now even *Shannon* was getting into it! "All we need is enough cord, and we can lower it down the hole and see if anyone's down there. Of course . . ." She paused, chewing on her thumbnail. "We'd need a computer to hook it up to. . . ."

"I could borrow my dad's laptop!" Derrick

exclaimed. "He never uses it, anyway. I'm sure he won't even miss it."

George looked over at Renee. Despite her objections, he could see from her face that even she was convinced.

"So, do we all agree to go on?"

"Aye," said Derrick.

"Aye," Renee agreed, shaking her head as if she couldn't believe it herself.

"Aye!" exclaimed Shannon, her eyes dancing with excitement as she scooted closer to the group. It looked like the old Shannon was back!

"That settles it, then," George said resolutely. "We're going back into the tunnels. Now let's make a plan."

TWO

DEAD MAN'S CHEST

"Okay, first thing we have to do," George said, unzipping his backpack, "is look at this." He gave everyone a glimpse of what was inside: the cat-o'-nine-tails whip they had taken from the skeleton in the tunnels.

"The map!"

Derrick said it so loud that a bunch of kids at nearby tables looked over at them. He lowered his voice.

"I totally forgot about it with the kidnapping and all."

George hadn't forgotten. They had risked too much to get it. *Snatch nine lives from a dead man's hand.* That was what Captain Kidd's clue had said. To their surprise, the "nine lives" had turned out to be a cat-o'-nine-tails, an old pirate whip with nine strands for nine times the lashing. They had found the whip in the hand of an ancient skeleton. They were sure that the next piece of Kidd's map was inside the handle, but they had agreed not to look at it until they were all together again.

"What are you waiting for?" cried Shannon impatiently. "Open it already!"

George looked around. The lunchroom was packed with other kids, which worried him. "I don't know if it's such a good idea to look at it here. There's too many people around, and someone is bound to see it. Besides, the map is pretty delicate. The parchment's so old, it could crumble into bits pretty easily."

"I know," Renee said suddenly. "The auditorium! Nobody's ever in there when the band isn't practicing." Renee would know: In addition to being the drummer for Shannon's band, the Diversions, she also was the lead percussionist in the school concert band.

The four of them quickly gulped down what was left of their lunches and snuck over to the auditorium. The huge room was empty, just as Renee had predicted. They took four seats in the front row, right in front of the orchestra pit. George pulled the cat-o'-nine-tails out of his backpack.

"Okay," he said, carefully twisting the cap at the end of the whip.

The cap popped off the end of the handle with a soft *whump*! A little wisp of stale-smelling air escaped. George stuck his finger in the handle and very carefully pulled the old piece of parchment out of it. Then he got up and walked toward the stage. The floorboards were about chest level from where they were standing in the orchestra pit. He unrolled it, careful not to apply too much pressure, and laid it flat on the stage. Derrick, Shannon, and Renee all followed and looked over his shoulder.

George felt a little chill. This was a piece of paper that was over three hundred years old. It had been owned by—maybe even *drawn* by—Captain Kidd! Even as he looked at the ancient black ink marks on the aged, brown parchment, George had trouble believing it was real.

"Whoa! What's that?" Derrick asked, pointing to a large dark blotch on the map.

"It must be a pond," Renee said. As part of a family of campers, she had looked at more maps than any of them.

"But that looks like a whole lake!" Shannon said. "Could that really be under New York?"

"Sure," replied George. "Why not? Those tunnels are between forty and a hundred feet underground. There's probably all kinds of stuff you'd never believe down there." He ran a finger over the map, looking for the room with the deadly obstacle course where they'd found the cat-o'-nine-tails. "Look," he said, pointing to a tunnel with a tiny cat drawn next to it. "The cat marks where we found the whip, and this flag must mark the room where we found the Jolly Roger! Too bad we didn't have this while we were looking!"

"Is that another clue?" Renee said, pointing to some ancient-looking writing in an ornately drawn box in a corner of the map.

"Yeah, it looks like it," said Derrick, who was leaning over the map from the top, looking at it upside down. "I can't read it. What does it say?"

"Let's see," George said, squinting to read the fancy script. "*If ye wish to continue the quest, ye must look deep inside a dead man's chest.*"

"Ewww!" Derrick said, making a face. "That's gross. I don't want to have to mug another skeleton. That last one gave me the creeps."

"We don't know that's what it means," said Shannon. "Remember, we thought 'nine lives' meant an actual cat, but it really meant the cat-o'-nine-tails. Maybe this clue is a kind of code as well."

"Why didn't Captain Kidd just say what he really meant?" Renee asked, putting her hands on her hips in frustration.

"Because if he made it too easy, then anyone could have found the treasure," said George, thinking the clue over in his head. "He wanted to make sure whoever found the treasure actually *earned* it."

"Hey, wait a minute," Renee said. "Where's the X?"

All their eyes returned to the map at once. Renee was right. The first map had had a big X on it, and X had marked the spot where they found Captain Kidd's journal. But there was no X on this map.

"How are we supposed to find the next map if there's no X?" Shannon asked.

George thought it over. "There's not always an X," he said after a few moments. "There was one on the first map, but that didn't lead to the next map, just to Kidd's journal. The journal led us to the next map, but there was no X to show where it was. We had to solve the riddle to find the map, so that's probably what we're going to have to do here."

"Which means we've got to find the 'dead man' from this riddle and look in his chest," Shannon pointed out. "It doesn't sound too hard. We just have to *find* the skeleton first."

"Hey, I just thought of something," Derrick chimed in. "What if this skeleton is on the other side of the lake? How are we going to get across it?"

They all looked at one another blankly. They hadn't thought of that.

"Of course!" Renee exclaimed suddenly. "My family's got a rubber blow-up raft. We used it when we went white-water rafting on vacation last summer."

"Can you sneak it out of the house without anyone noticing?" George asked.

"No problem!" Renee said brightly. "Remember the big cases I put my drums in when I have to move them?"

George winced. How could he forget? Shannon and Renee's rock band, the Diversions, had played at his birthday party—until the cops had come after someone complained about the noise. No one at the party had been very upset to hear them stop. "Um, sure," he replied.

"I'll just tell my parents that the Diversions are practicing at your house this weekend. But I'll put the raft in the biggest case instead of my bass drum!"

George nodded. "Sounds like a good plan," he agreed.

"Any idea on where to look for the skeleton?" Derrick asked. They all looked at George. They really did think of him as their captain, George realized with a little stab of pride.

"Well, first we should ask Paul if he's seen a skeleton like this," he said. "We can go into the tunnels tomorrow and find him."

"And bring him his Oreos," Shannon said, remembering the treat she had promised Paul. He had never tasted Oreos before they'd given him some, and now he couldn't wait to get more.

"I almost forgot about the Oreos," Derrick said. "Didn't you use them all up making a trail after Roulain kidnapped you?"

Shannon nodded. "Yeah. I'm going to have to buy another two bags. I hope I have enough money."

George dug into his pocket and found a five-dollar bill. "Here," he said. "We might as well pay for it out of my birthday fund." George had gotten birthday cards from all of his relatives who lived too far away to attend his birthday party. All in all, he had received almost forty dollars. They had already used some of the money to get them out of another jam.

Derrick laughed. "That's pretty funny," he said.

"What?" George asked.

"Your birthday was the whole start of this adventure," Derrick explained. "And now your birthday money is paying for it!"

George stepped onto the bus and put his MetroCard in the slot near the driver. For many kids in public school, living in New York City meant you didn't have a yellow school bus come and pick you up every morning and take you home in the afternoon. Instead George had to take the same bus that many adults rode to work. The machine spit out George's card, and the little screen said in green, digital letters that George had only one ride left. He would have to mention this to his dad, who bought special discount student MetroCards for George and gave him new ones whenever they ran out.

Usually Derrick rode the same bus with George, and they always got a kick out of the funny sight of businesspeople wearing suits with sneakers. But today Derrick was staying late at school for extra help with math, so George pushed his way through the crowd and took a seat next to a plump lady reading the *New York Post*.

There were a couple of stops until George would be getting off the bus, so he reached into his backpack and pulled out *Famous Pirates of England*, another one of the books his father had given him for his birthday. As he paged through the old drawings of famous pirates like Samuel "Black" Bellamy, Mary Read, and Blackbeard, George suddenly realized that he hadn't really let his father know how much he enjoyed the old books. They had been especially valuable in the course of his recent adventures, although he couldn't tell his dad *that*. But he could tell him how much he liked them. He thought that would be enough.

George got off the bus at his stop and walked the half block to his house. He took out his house key and opened the door.

"Hi, Dad," he called out. "I'm home." He saw his dad's head turn from his usual spot in his easy chair. But another head turned as well—a woman's head. She had long brown hair that was tied in the back in a loose bun. George stopped dead in his tracks. They *never* had guests over!

"George," his father said, rising from his easy chair and motioning to the strange woman, who was wearing a cardigan sweater and had thin, wire-rimmed glasses. A plain brown skirt went all the way down to her ankles. "I'd like to introduce you to Professor Kira Trenov. She's a visiting professor at my college, all the way from Oxford University in England."

"Nice to meet you," George mumbled, shaking her hand. So much for getting a chance to have a talk with his dad.

"And very nice to meet *you*." She had a peculiar accent, not British like their neighbors, the St. Johns. It was a little harsher, a little more clipped.

"Professor Trenov is also a professor of Litarian history," his father went on. "In fact, she originally comes from Litaria. . . ." George nodded. That would explain the accent.

"And I couldn't resist the chance to pick the brain of one of the world's leading experts on Litaria," Professor Trenov finished for him, smiling widely. George knew his father knew a lot about the small eastern European country of Litaria, but he'd never heard anyone call him an *expert* before.

"That's nice," George said.

"I was hoping that Professor Trenov would join us for dinner," his father continued.

"Why, how lovely! I'd be delighted," she replied, clapping.

"George, why don't you set the table while I get started in the kitchen?" his father asked. George put his backpack on the stairs and went into the kitchen.

The dinner was average van Gelder fare: baked chicken, instant mashed potatoes, and frozen green beans warmed in the microwave. But Professor Trenov acted like it was the greatest meal ever made. George thought that was a little odd. Why was she being so nice to his dad?

George barely listened to the boring conversation the two adults had about Litaria, but they both seemed very into it. In fact, Professor Trenov seemed to hang on his father's every word.

"Professor van Gelder, I would love to hear about how you researched the article you wrote for *Litaria Today* magazine," Professor Trenov said between bites of chicken. "You know, the one about how local villages preserved true Litarian traditions while the country was occupied by Soviet troops."

George's father began a long explanation about

how the Litarian people had persevered under
Soviet occupation after World War II. While his
father was talking, George studied Professor Trenov.
He had a funny feeling about her. It was a pretty big
coincidence that some professor would come
around to his house, asking questions about Litaria
at a time like this. After all, Litaria was the country
where the Eye of Eternity had originally come from.

Holy smoke! All at once George remembered
that he and his friends had seen a woman, dressed
all in black, skulking around the tunnels about a
week before. At first George had thought it might
be his neighbor, Mrs. St. John. But he couldn't
figure out why she would be down there. As far as
George could tell, his three friends, the homeless
people who lived down there, the mystery woman,
and Roulain were the only ones who even knew
that the tunnels existed. But now, as he looked
across the table at Professor Trenov, George realized that she was almost the same size as Mrs. St.
John. Could *she* be the skulker?

George watched Professor Trenov carefully. She
was smiling at George's father, drinking in every
word he was saying about Litaria.

I don't know if I like this, George thought. *I'm
going to have to keep an eye on her.*

George excused himself and went upstairs to his

room. He pulled out Captain Kidd's journal from its hiding place behind his clothes hamper. He sat down on his bed to read, but he kept thinking about the stranger, Kira Trenov. If she *was* the skulker in the tunnels, then maybe she had figured out that there was an entrance to the tunnels from the van Gelders' house. The house was a registered historical building, after all, and it was no secret that it had belonged to Captain Kidd. What if she was just waiting until his father left the room so she could sneak around the house, looking for a way into the tunnels? Sure, the notion was far-fetched, but could George take that chance?

Taking the journal with him, George quietly went out to the staircase and hid on the upstairs landing. From there he could clearly hear the two of them talking downstairs. He tried to read some of the journal, but it was hard to concentrate when he had to listen to the two of them drone on about Litarian history until ten forty-five, when Professor Trenov finally left.

Well, at least nothing suspicious had happened, but George didn't think he had ever been so bored in his entire life!

"I can't believe how long this is taking!" Shannon grumbled while Derrick finished setting up his plan to keep their rope hidden. He had dug out a section of the wall of the shaft that they used to descend into the tunnels. Then he coiled the end of the rope and placed it in the hole he had created. The finishing touch was a flat piece of board he had worked on at home the night before. Derrick had glued clumps of dirt on the wood so when he wedged it into place over the hole, no one could even tell it was there.

"We had a deal, remember?" Derrick said. "It's too dangerous to use George's basement unless we hide the rope."

"I know," said Shannon. "But between this and the time we spent attaching the latch to the trapdoor and scouting the tunnel with the web cam, we've wasted almost an entire hour."

"We'll just have to watch the time," Derrick responded with a shrug.

"I'm on that," George said, pressing the buttons on the sides of his watch. It suddenly glowed blue-green in the dark.

"Just make sure you're careful when you turn that thing on," Renee warned. "We don't want to be spotted." Even though the watch's light was very dim, the tunnels seemed even darker after George shut it off.

"Ow!" Derrick stifled his outburst as best he

could. "I stubbed my toe on this stupid log. Who thought it would be a good idea to put a log in a tunnel, anyway? Can we put on our brights so we don't walk into something else?" "Brights" was what Paul called the lights on the helmets they used.

"Well, okay. But just one of them," George said. "And be ready to turn it off again in a hurry!" Derrick snapped on his light, and everyone walked in the small pool of light that it cast on the ground before them.

The four kids made their way through the tunnel. When they got to the fork, they could hear the sound of machines humming from the branch of the tunnel that went off to their right.

"That must be Roulain's men," whispered George. "Good thing we're not going that way. But be very, very quiet!"

They tiptoed out of the section of tunnel that led from George's basement, moving down the tunnel to their left. They crept silently until they came to the spot where the tunnel opened up into the floor of an abandoned subway tunnel. One by one they hoisted themselves up into the large, dark tunnel.

"This place still gives me the creeps," Derrick said. The light from his helmet reflected weakly off the old, dull subway tracks. He shivered.

"Careful what you say," Shannon said. "This is Paul's home you're talking about."

Once they were all safely on solid ground, George led them in the direction of the abandoned shantytown. They still sometimes found Paul hanging around here.

"Paul!" called Shannon, reaching into her backpack. She had brought two bags of Oreos for him, just as she had promised.

"Shhh!" George said. "Not so loud! We don't want to attract any attention if Roulain's men are still down here."

"Sorry," Shannon whispered.

"Derrick, flash your light," George said. "Maybe he'll see that."

All four of them stood stock-still, not making a sound and listening as hard as they could. They couldn't hear anything except for the very soft ticking of George's watch. *Tick. Tick. Tick.*

Suddenly, they heard a voice in the dark.

"What are *you* doing here?"

Three
MUTINY

"Aaah!"

They were all so surprised by the sound of Paul's voice, they screamed in shock.

"Jeez, Paul," George said, lowering his voice and looking around. He listened for sounds of Leroy's thugs approaching. But he heard nothing. "You scared the life out of us. How did you sneak up on us like that?"

"I know how to get around down here," Paul said. There was a funny edge to his voice. "I don't make a sound. But I could hear *you* three tunnels away."

Paul regarded the four of them with an almost angry expression. *He sounds upset,* George thought. *Maybe it's because we never gave him his Oreos.* Shannon was supposed to have brought Paul two bags of the cookies, but before she could meet up with him, she'd been kidnapped by Roulain's thugs.

George mouthed the word *Oreos* to Shannon, who immediately took off her backpack and unzipped it, taking out two jumbo-size bags of blue cellophane.

"Paul, I brought you the Oreos," Shannon said. "Two bags, just like I promised."

There was a moment of silence.

"You . . . you did?" Paul sounded surprised. "But I didn't think you were coming back."

"What? What made you think that?" Now George was the one who sounded surprised.

"After I helped you look for Shannon, you disappeared. I thought maybe you wouldn't come back because of what happened."

They were all stunned. No one knew what to say. Suddenly, it dawned on George: After he'd stumbled on the elevator to Roulain's apartment and the others had tried to find him aboveground, Paul must have felt like they had abandoned him. Paul probably thought that George and his friends had used him to navigate the tunnels and then just taken off, never intending to honor Shannon's promise to bring him the Oreos. That wasn't what had happened—but Paul didn't know that!

George opened his mouth to explain. But it appeared that Shannon, Derrick, and Renee had the same realization as George. Then they all started talking at once.

"We were kidnapped . . ."

". . . held prisoner . . ."

". . . Roulain's apartment . . ."

". . . where he lives . . ."

". . . on the dayside . . ."

". . . had to escape . . ."

". . . no time to get back . . ."

Somehow in all the confusion Paul managed to figure out what they were all trying to tell him.

"You always meant to come back?"

"Of course, silly," Shannon said, holding out the Oreos. "A promise is a promise."

Paul was silent again, but when he spoke, his voice sounded funny. "No one ever kept a promise to me before."

George and his friends looked at one another, considering what Paul had said. They hadn't realized how much their promise had meant to him.

"Well, this won't be the last time," George said.

Paul tore one of the cellophane bags open and jammed three Oreos into his mouth at once. He didn't look mad anymore, but he had a faraway look in his eyes as he chewed, like he was still trying to figure something out.

"I think I need to tell you something," he began uncertainly.

"Go ahead," urged George.

"Yeah," said Shannon. "We're friends. You can tell us anything."

Paul nodded slowly. "You remember when you first saw me, when I was captured by Leroy? And then later you wanted to know if I gave him anything."

"Sure," George said. "You gave him the old rock with the funny-looking letters on it. We've been trying to figure out what that could be, but we haven't come up with anything."

"Well . . . that wasn't true."

George and his friends gasped in surprise, and Paul looked down at his feet. "What I really found was an old piece of paper," he began. "I didn't know what it was, but now I think it's one of your maps."

George looked at Paul silently. "Really?" he asked after a moment. "Paul, why didn't you tell us that before?"

Paul shrugged. "I just . . . didn't trust you." He met George's eyes. "People aren't nice here like they must be on the dayside. I thought you wanted something from me, just like Leroy's men."

George shook his head. "We're not like Leroy's thugs, Paul." Now it was George who had an angry edge in his voice. They had wasted time poring over Captain Kidd's journal looking for a mention of a rock with markings on it. But now it seemed that Paul had made the story up because he didn't trust them! George tried to tell himself that they shouldn't be too hard on Paul because of the harsh circumstances he lived under. But he couldn't help feeling angry about the time they'd lost on a wild-goose chase.

"What did it look like, Paul? Do you remember?" Shannon asked. She sounded like she was annoyed by this development, too.

"It had weird marks in the corner. Like this."

Paul started drawing in the damp dirt of the cave floor with his finger. Derrick focused his bright on the spot as Paul finished etching "IV."

George could hear all of his friends sucking in their breath. They all knew what this meant. IV was the Roman numeral for the number 4. That meant Roulain had the fourth map. If Roulain had figured out the map's clue, then he knew where to find the Eye of Eternity.

"Well, that's it, then," Derrick said dejectedly. "It's all over. Roulain's won."

"Yeah. He's got map four, all right." Renee kicked the dirt with the toe of her shoe.

"What's wrong?" Paul asked. He sounded confused. "I just wanted to help. Why are you so mad?"

"We're not mad at you, Paul." Shannon sighed. The fact that Paul had lied to them seemed like less of a big deal now that they'd learned that Roulain had the fourth map. *That* was something to really get mad about! "We're just *mad*. Leroy's going to beat us to the treasure, and there's nothing we can do about it."

"Oh," Paul replied quietly.

"I don't know, guys," George said. "It might not be so bad."

"Oh, come on, George!" Shannon exploded. "Remember how we saw all that equipment Roulain brought down here? That's because he knows where the treasure is. He's probably digging it up right now."

"Yeah, George. He'll get at that treasure a lot quicker with his fancy equipment than we ever could," Renee pointed out.

"And now that he knows he's so close, there's no way he'll leave it unguarded," Derrick added. They had heard the sounds of Roulain's men working their machines, and now they knew why.

"But that can't be it," George insisted stubbornly. He had talked them out of quitting before. Maybe he could do it again. "It can't be that easy. Captain Kidd—"

"Captain Kidd, Captain Kidd, *Captain Kidd*!" Shannon's voice rose. "You're obsessed with Captain Kidd, George. But he must not have been as clever as you think, because the bad guys are going to get the treasure!"

George was stunned. He saw Shannon's eyes flash in the darkness.

"The game is *over*," she said with finality. "We're not playing anymore."

Paul nodded. "You really don't belong down here, anyway." It wasn't the first time he had said that to them.

George looked at the faces of the others and saw that he had lost them. "Okay, then," he said finally with a deep sigh. "If that's how you all feel."

"It is," Renee said. "Now, we should get going. I've got some homework to do."

"Yeah, and I might be able to catch the end of *The Simpsons*," Derrick admitted.

"Well, let's stop talking and get out of here before anything else bad happens to us," Shannon said, starting back down the tunnel. George stood in the tunnel for a moment, watching them go. He couldn't believe they'd gotten this far all for nothing. Reluctantly he glanced at Paul and followed his friends. Paul trailed after them, munching his Oreos.

When they came to the opening that led down to the shaft under George's basement, they stopped to say good-bye to Paul.

"I'm glad you liked the Oreos, Paul," Shannon said, shaking his hand just like they were adults. "Maybe sometime we can bring you more."

"Bye, Paul," Derrick mumbled, shaking his hand,

too. "Take care of yourself down here."

"Are you sure you don't want to come dayside?" Renee asked. "There are places you could go, places you could stay. . . ."

But Paul just shook his head. "Uh-uh," he said. "Leroy may be down here, but dayside is *scary*."

Renee looked like she was going to push the issue but then just hugged him quickly. Paul seemed a bit uncomfortable. "Stay safe!" she whispered as Derrick pulled the end of the rope out of its hiding place.

They climbed up the rope one at a time. First went Shannon, then Renee, then Derrick. As Derrick was climbing up the rope, George made up his mind. He whispered something to Paul that the others couldn't hear.

Once they were all in the basement, they coiled up the rope and latched the trapdoor in case Roulain or anyone else tried to climb up. They took their time, since they had left the tunnels earlier than they planned and were in no danger of George's dad coming home anytime soon. He was next door playing bridge with the St. Johns, like he did every Tuesday night.

When they had finished moving all the boxes of books back into place, Derrick asked George what he had said to Paul.

"Nothing," he said. "Nothing important."

George hoped that Derrick believed him, because he wasn't telling the truth. He had said something important to Paul, but he couldn't let Derrick—or any of the others—find out what it was.

Derrick looked like he was going to press George on the issue, but then he just shrugged and followed everyone else upstairs to call their parents.

It was awkward to say good-bye that night. Even though they knew they would see one another at school the next day, it felt like they were saying good-bye for good.

"Don't forget to look after my 'drums,'" Renee said to George on her way out the door. Renee's parents had gone on a short hike after dropping her off at George's that afternoon. Since Shannon's father's car wasn't big enough, they had to leave her drum cases in George's basement.

"No problem," George said, secretly grateful that she had to leave the drum case behind because that meant she was also leaving the raft.

After they were all gone, George went upstairs, threw his dirty clothes in the hamper, and washed up before changing into his pajamas. It was one of the first times he had cleaned up properly after a pirate adventure, that was for sure.

When his dad came home, George was already in bed, reading *Cutthroat Pirates of the South Seas.*

"Well, this is a surprise," his dad said. "Your friends have all gone home early. Was there a mutiny?"

George's dad was trying to make a joke. But George didn't think it was very funny.

Four

ALONE

"Why, what an absolutely wonderful idea!"

The familiar accent of Kira Trenov stopped George in his tracks. He had been bounding down the stairs, on his way to the front door. He had told his dad he was going over to Derrick's house, but he was actually planning to sneak back around and in through his own basement window.

What was *she* doing here? And on a *Saturday*, too!

"George!" his father said brightly. "Come say hello to Professor Trenov."

George trudged slowly down the steps and walked up to Professor Trenov.

"Hi," he mumbled.

"How nice to see you again, George," she said. "I'm sorry to hear you won't be joining us today."

"We're going to the Museum of Eastern European History," his dad said with a broad smile, as if this were the most exciting news in the world. "They're hosting a traveling exhibit of Litarian artifacts. Kira's even getting us in at a discount."

Kira? That was the first time he'd heard his father call Professor Trenov by her first name. George looked at her through narrowed eyes. She was winning over his father's trust, all right. If she was really after the Eye, wouldn't that be part of her plan?

"I thought you and your friends might like to come along, George," his dad went on. "Isn't Shannon doing a report on Litaria?"

"Really?" Professor Trenov rolled her *r*'s when she said that. She looked at George with interest.

At first George had no idea what his father was talking about. Then he remembered. George's dad had interrupted them the other night while they were investigating Captain Kidd's journal. Shannon had faked an interest in Litaria, pretending she was doing a school report, to distract him. Predictably, it had worked like a charm. George's dad was so happy to talk about Litaria that he'd never noticed the journal. And even better, they'd learned everything that George's dad knew about the Eye of Eternity.

"Uh, I don't think so," George replied. "Shannon, um, handed that report in yesterday."

"Oh, that's a shame," Professor Trenov said. "I'm sure if she was still doing her research, she would have liked to see this." She pulled out a small metal object that was hanging on a chain around her neck. It looked really old, like it belonged in a museum itself.

"I had forgotten about that. You'll like the story behind this, George." His father was beaming, and George couldn't bear to disappoint him.

"What's the story?" he asked, wishing they would hurry up. He wanted to get down into the tunnels as soon as possible, but he had to admit the thing looked pretty interesting. It had a funny shape, like a cross between an oval and a four-sided diamond. George kept looking at it. It was easier than looking Professor Trenov in the eye.

"Well, it's really more of a folktale," Professor Trenov began. "I'm not sure if anyone who didn't grow up in Litaria would ever have heard it. This seal was originally owned by a Litarian duke named Sergei, who is one of my distant ancestors. In 1701 the king of Litaria sent Sergei on a very special mission across the sea. Before he left, he gave his wife this, which he had used to seal his letters."

Professor Trenov arched an eyebrow at George, which made her look quite sinister. "You are familiar with this practice?" she asked.

George nodded. In history class they had read about how in that era, wealthy people used melted wax to close their letters. They had individual seals made that depicted their coats of arms, and they pressed the seals into the hot wax. That way the recipient knew who had sent the letter.

"Well," she continued, "Sergei gave the seal to his beloved and said, 'I will not need this seal on my journey because any time I could spend writing you a letter would be better spent returning to you sooner.' It is a very romantic story."

George's father was clearly captivated. Professor Trenov continued.

"But Sergei never returned from this voyage. And his wife wore the seal around her neck after that. She never took it off because she believed he might still return someday. She died with it still around her neck. It has been passed down in our family from generation to generation ever since. And now I am the one honored to wear it."

"I think George would be more interested in the *rest* of the story," his father urged.

Kira chuckled. "Oh, of course he would! What do young boys care about romance? They want to hear about *adventure*! I must warn you, though, this is where the story is probably more legend than fact. The story goes that Sergei was to have a fateful meeting with the most dangerous pirate in the world . . . Captain Kidd!"

George suddenly snapped to attention. Had she just said *Captain Kidd*?

"Ho, ho, George!" his dad said. "Finally something in this story for you, huh?"

"Captain Kidd wasn't a pirate," George said. "He was a *privateer*. There's a difference."

"That may be," Professor Trenov said slowly, sizing George up. "But he still is rumored to have come into possession of our country's greatest treasure: the Eye of Eternity. According to the legend, Sergei's mission was to get back the Eye for Litaria. Captain Kidd had actually sent word to the Litarian king that he should send an emissary to retrieve the diamond. But instead Kidd lured him into a trap and killed him. Which is why Sergei never returned to Litaria."

"No way! Captain Kidd never would have done that!" George could feel his face flushing with anger.

"George!" his father said sharply. "Mind your manners!"

"That's okay, Peter," Professor Trenov said. "The fault is mine. I've clearly insulted George's hero."

"Well, we should get going, anyway," George's father said, frowning at George. "Do you want to walk us to the bus stop?" he asked.

"Um—no," George stammered. "I forgot I was supposed to . . . um, call Shannon before I go."

"Okay. Well, just make sure you're home by five o'clock. I thought it would be nice for the three of us to go to dinner," his dad said as he held the door open for Professor Trenov. "Kira knows a lovely place in Little Litaria." George rolled his eyes. New York City had lots of ethnic neighborhoods, like Chinatown and Little Italy, but he had never heard of Little Litaria before. But if it had anything to do with Litaria, of *course* his father knew about it!

"Don't forget to lock up when you go," Peter van Gelder said as he closed the door.

"I won't," George called after his father, but it was all he could do to keep from shouting it in anger. Where did Professor Trenov get the nerve to go spreading stories like that about Captain Kidd?

But as George's anger faded, he had another thought. If Professor Trenov knew of the connection between Captain Kidd and Litaria, then maybe she really *was* the skulker in the tunnels. It was certainly a pretty big coincidence, and the more George thought about it, the more all the evidence pointed to Professor Trenov being involved in the hunt for the Eye of Eternity.

George waited another fifteen minutes, watching through the window to make sure they didn't come back. Then he headed for the basement. At least he didn't have to sneak through the window now.

But as he walked down to the basement, he was still angry about what Professor Trenov had said about Captain Kidd. George didn't trust her, not one bit. And when had she started calling his father by his *first* name?

It took George longer than he'd thought to tie the spare piece of rope around the raft. Even folded up, with all the air out of it, the raft was pretty big and bulky. First he thought he could just drop it down the shaft and then pick it up when he got down there. But it was heavy and would probably make a loud *thud* when it landed. George didn't want to attract any attention. It was bad enough that he would be going down the shaft without Shannon's web cam to scout ahead. He'd have to be very careful.

Even though the others had decided to quit the adventure, George couldn't bring himself to just give up. Even though things looked pretty bleak— with Roulain having stolen the fourth map and all— George couldn't shake the feeling that the game wasn't over yet. Captain Kidd was too clever for the treasure to be found so easily. All George had to do was find proof that they could still beat Roulain to the Eye of Eternity, and he was sure he'd be able to talk his friends back into being pyrates.

But for now, it was all up to him. And Paul, who had agreed to meet George down in the tunnels.

George took a deep breath as he pulled open the trapdoor and smelled the cold, damp air of the tunnels. "Better face it, George," he said to himself. "You're on your own now. It's a whole new ball game."

He tied the end of the spare rope to one of the belt loops on his pants. When he got to the bottom, he could just pull the raft down behind him. Perfect. He then tied the other length of rope to his waist—it was anchored to a heavy carton of books—and started lowering himself down the shaft.

"Steady, George. Nice and slow."

Oh, great, he thought. *Now I'm talking to myself. I'm the only one left in my pyrate gang, so I've only got* myself *to order around!*

George lowered himself hand over hand, inching down the shaft a little at a time. For some reason, it seemed harder when he was by himself. His arms were sore from the strain, and he was panting like he'd just finished running a race. He'd never realized how much having friends with you could make a hard job seem easier.

Hand over hand. Hand over hand.

George stopped just above where the shaft opened out over the tunnel below. He strained his ears as hard as he could, but the only sound he could hear was his own labored breathing.

Okay, George. Here we go.

George let go of the rope and dropped down. He landed in a crouch and immediately lifted his head. He looked left . . . looked right . . . and saw . . .

Nothing. There was nobody around.

George let out his breath in a deep sigh. He hadn't even realized he'd been holding it.

Untying the spare rope from around his belt loop, George gave it a hard tug. He felt resistance, but he also felt it give a little as the raft moved across the floor of his basement forty feet above. He yanked it again and felt it move a little more.

George stopped to catch his breath. This was harder than he'd thought! For a moment he considered leaving the raft behind. He wasn't even sure he'd need to go out on the underground lake. It all depended on where the skeleton with the next map was.

Better bring it along just in case, he thought. *If I need it and don't have it, then I'll have wasted the whole day. But if I've got it with me, then I'm prepared either way.*

George gave the rope one more yank, the hardest yet, and felt the raft skid toward the opening. Then the rope went slack in his hand, and George prepared to catch the falling raft in his arms. But as it raced down the shaft toward him, George realized that it was falling too fast for him to handle by himself.

George dashed away from the opening of the shaft just in time.

Thwapp!

The sound was much louder than George would have thought. He crouched down behind the log that stuck out of the floor, waiting to see if the sound would bring anyone to check it out. He tried to keep quiet, but he was breathing heavily from running out of the raft's path, and his heart was thudding in his chest. After a moment he got his breathing under control and listened for the sound of someone approaching. But no one came.

After a few minutes had passed and George was sure no one was coming to investigate, he got up and secured the end of the descent rope in the hiding place Derrick had rigged up. He thought of his friend and how much he wished Derrick were here right now.

But he's not, he reminded himself. *It's just me. One lonely pyrate. Me against the world. Just like Captain Kidd.*

For the first time since his friends had quit the quest, George wondered if he was doing the right thing. Could he really finish the treasure hunt without his friends? After all, he couldn't even handle the raft by himself. What else was going to happen that was easier for a group of friends to handle than one kid by himself?

And George had to admit, without his friends the tunnels looked a little darker. And a *lot* scarier.

Well, I'm here now, George thought. *I might as well try.*

He slung the spare rope over his shoulder, carrying the raft like a backpack, and started down the tunnel. He didn't get more than ten feet before he heard the buzzing of machinery. George crept very quietly to the end of the tunnel, where it opened up and split two ways. He peered around the corner.

Down the tunnel on the right George saw some dim light coming from far off. He could barely make out the sound of voices. It must be Roulain's men, using their fancy equipment to dig for the treasure. George and his friends had heard them working down there before, but now that George knew what they were up to, he wanted to get a good look. He crept down the right branch of the tunnel, in the direction of the noises.

It took George a while to make his way down the tunnel without a light. To him it seemed like forever. Eventually he came to a slight bend in the tunnel, and the light seemed much brighter just beyond it. The hum of the machinery was much louder now. It was starting to make George's head ache.

George got down low to the ground and peeked

around the bend in the tunnel. He didn't think the men would be able to see him, because he was crouching in the dark shadows while they were under the bright electric lights. He watched them work for a couple of seconds. One man was using a big mechanical device that looked like a jack-hammer to loosen the hard-packed dirt. Another was shoveling out the dirt loosened by the jack-hammer. It was piled up on the sides of the hole they were digging. There was all sorts of other equipment tossed in a sloppy pile. One piece had a disk at one end of a long handle, and George real-ized it was a metal detector. Another item looked like the metal detector, but instead of a disk at the end it had a long, narrow metal cone with a red light on it. *It's probably some kind of fancy jewel loca-tor or something,* George thought, his heart sinking in his chest. Seeing all that equipment made George realize just how far Roulain was willing to go to find the Eye of Eternity.

The piles of dirt were big, George noticed. They must have been digging for a while. One of the men was resting against a piece of log that was sticking out of the dirt floor. He looked exhausted, and his T-shirt and jeans were smeared with dirt and dust. *I'll have to mention that log to Derrick,* George thought. *He'll be glad to know that the one he keeps stubbing his toe on isn't the only one down here.*

"They can't be in the right place," George muttered to himself, trying to make himself believe. "They just *can't* be."

He watched them for a few more moments and then quietly tiptoed back the way he'd come. He passed the tunnel that went back to his house and headed in the direction of the abandoned subway tunnel.

He walked up the tunnel a ways, the buzzing sound of the mechanical dirt-loosener fading behind him. Eventually, he squeezed through a narrow opening and came out on the abandoned subway line. Old, unused train tracks stretched off into the dark, lonely tunnels. This was where George and his friends had first met Paul and where George had told Paul to meet him today.

Sure enough, there was Paul, leaning against the old subway platform, waiting for him. He smiled when he saw George, and George noticed little pieces of Oreos in his teeth. *I'll have to remember to bring him a toothbrush,* George thought. *And some toothpaste.* If he and his friends were going to introduce Paul to sweets, they owed it to him to look after his dental hygiene. And nothing messed up your teeth like Oreos.

"I didn't know if you were coming," Paul said, "since the others aren't coming back. You're brave to come down by yourself. Especially with Leroy's men over there."

"Yeah, I saw them, too," George replied. "But you know, I'm not really all by myself. You're here."

Paul smiled again. It seemed he liked being part of a group. Not that there was much of a group to be a part of anymore . . .

"What are you going to do now?" Paul asked.

"Well, that's where you can really help me," George replied. He pulled out both of Captain Kidd's maps and showed them to Paul. "We're right here, see? And we're going to go back here"— George pointed to where the tunnels branched off, where they had found the cat-o'-nine-tails—"but we're not going back up there. We're going to stay in this tunnel here"—his finger traced the path of the tunnel to the east—"and follow it down toward this big thing. It looks to me like a lake. Do you know where that is?"

Paul nodded gravely. "Don't like it there. Big water's there. Don't like the big water."

"That's okay, Paul," George said, putting a reassuring hand on Paul's shoulder. "You won't have to go over the big water. I'll do that by myself." He patted the raft. "But what I really want to know," George continued, "is if you've seen any skeletons down this way?"

"I *don't* go down that way," Paul said, with a little edge in his voice, like he was frustrated because George wasn't listening to him. "The big water is down that way. *I don't like the big water.*"

"Okay, okay," George said. He obviously wasn't going to get much help from Paul in finding the skeleton. Still, he was the only hope George had.

"Paul, I hope you'll help me look for the skeleton down here. We're going to go toward the big water, but I'm not going to make you go *in* it. Okay?"

Paul looked at George suspiciously. Then he nodded. "Okay. But no big water."

"All right," George said. "No big water."

Just as they were setting off, George noticed a broken piece of board lying in the cinders under the subway tracks. He jogged over and picked it up. It was splintered at one end, but the other end was still in one piece. It was flat and just thick enough for the purpose he intended. "I think I've just found myself a paddle," he said.

Paul led George down the subway tunnel to the spot where they had discovered another of Captain Kidd's tunnels. They moved on past the branch they had followed to find the cat-o'-nine-tails.

George shivered as he remembered the quicksand they had stumbled on. He hoped there wouldn't be anything *that* dangerous down the new tunnel, but who knew what surprises there might be?

The two walked silently, George looking over his shoulder every couple of feet to make sure no one was following them. After they passed the area of the tunnel he was familiar with, George noticed that the ground slanted down at a slight angle. It made sense, he thought, that this underground lake—or whatever it was—would be deeper underground than some of the other tunnels.

George sniffed at the air. It smelled damp. It *felt* damp.

It was colder, too. He could see his breath in front of him when he exhaled.

"Wait."

George stopped. Paul was leading because it was safer to travel without lights on and Paul knew how to walk around tunnels in the dark better than George did.

"I feel something here."

George let Paul direct his hand to a section of wall on their left. There was a thin opening, just wide enough for them to get in and out, but it would be a very tight fit for an adult.

"Paul, I'm going to have to use my bright. You'd better close your eyes."

Paul covered his eyes with his hands, and George turned on the light at the front of his helmet. Just past the opening was a small room, about ten feet by ten feet, cut out of the rock. In the corner was a skeleton, leaning against the wall as if hastily propped there.

George felt a chill. Was it fright? Excitement? Or both?

"I think that's it!" he said excitedly. He squeezed through the tight opening and moved toward the skeleton, but something held him back. What was it? In his excitement, it took George a second to realize that the folded-up raft, which was still slung over his shoulder, was too big to fit through the small opening.

"I guess I'll have to leave this here," George mumbled impatiently, tossing it farther down the tunnel in the direction of the damp smell. "But it looks like I might not need it after all!"

George crept back into the small room and approached the skeleton. It looked creepy in the pale light of his bright, and his breath looked eerie, like little wisps of mist.

George sensed something over his shoulder and almost jumped a mile straight up. But it was just Paul creeping up behind him.

"If Captain Kidd was a good guy," Paul said, "why are there so many skeletons?"

"It's kind of complicated," George responded absentmindedly. He was looking at the skeleton's chest. There should be something inside its rib cage. That's what the clue had said: *Look deep inside a dead man's chest.* But nothing was there.

The skull grinned evilly at George, like it was mocking him.

"Maybe this is the wrong skeleton," George said, consulting the map again. He doubted it, though. There was even a little smudge of ink in this section on the map.

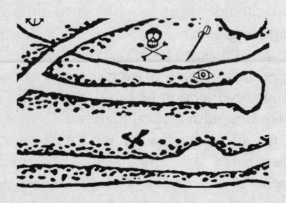

It had probably been an X to show that this was the right spot, but it had been worn away by time.

than the other bones, which had all yellowed with age. In fact, looking at it closely, George thought this one wasn't bone at all. It looked like it might be ivory.

"That's got to be it," George said. He pulled the cat-o'-nine-tails out of his backpack. The "bone" was roughly the same size as the handle of the whip. The perfect size for hiding a map.

"Ha!" George exclaimed, reaching for the bone. It felt smooth and cool, and when he gave it a tug, it fell into his hand easily. *Who needs a whole pyrate crew?*

Suddenly, there was a deep rumble outside the little room. George looked around wildly. What was going on? He looked back at the skeleton. Then he noticed that the piece of ivory he'd just taken had been held in place with a little leather strap. He'd seen that kind of leather strap before. In Captain Kidd's other booby traps.

Uh-oh.

"Run!" he shouted.

Five

BIG WATER

Dust and rocks were falling from the ceiling. It was hard to see, even with the bright on. George grabbed Paul by the shoulders and pushed him through the narrow opening.

George squeezed through behind him. He saw the fear on Paul's face. George seized his wrist and started to run.

"Aaah!"

A huge chunk of rock fell right in front of them, almost crushing them. George turned around and ran the other way, pulling Paul behind him. They ran down the tunnel, through the dust and the rocks, following the tunnel down. Several small rocks hit George on the arms and shoulders as they ran past. Some just stung, but others really hurt. The tunnel curved down to the right, and it was hard to see ahead of them. They kept running, too scared to notice that the dust was clearing and the rumbling had stopped.

They turned a corner and kept running and—

"Aaah!"

George pulled up short when he heard Paul scream. Then he saw why.

"Big water!"

Laid out in front of them was the most amazing sight George had ever seen. A giant underground lake filled an enormous cavern so big that George couldn't see the edges, even with his bright. The water looked black in the darkness. It lapped at their feet, touching the toes of George's sneakers. If they hadn't stopped when Paul screamed, they would have run right in.

George could see why Paul was so scared of the big water. It looked like a giant pool of liquid darkness.

"Don't like big water!" Paul cried. His voice broke and sounded thin.

"It's okay, Paul. I think the rock slide has stopped." George listened. He couldn't hear it anymore. "Let's go back and see."

Paul nodded shakily and turned around.

The two of them trudged up the tunnel, back in the direction of the room with the skeleton. As they neared it, they had to step over piles of rock and dirt, the remains of the rock slide that had almost buried them alive.

As they approached the opening to the room where the skeleton lay, George had a bad feeling about what they'd find. When they rounded the corner, his bad feeling got worse.

The tunnel was completely blocked. Rocks, dirt, and dust were piled all the way to the ceiling. There was no way to get past it. No way out.

George stood and stared at the blocked tunnel. He could hardly believe this was really happening. He looked back at the map again. Had he missed something? Then he saw it. The smudge. In his excitement George had assumed that it was an X, but now he realized that it had probably been an eye, the warning of a booby trap.

If the others were here, you never would have forgotten about the eyes, George scolded himself. *Someone would have remembered. Someone would have thought of it. Maybe you're not so good on your own after all.*

Then he turned and looked at Paul, who had a look of panic in his eyes.

"What are we going to do, George?" he asked.

There was only one thing they could do. "I'm sorry, Paul, but we're going to have to go over the big water."

George took a deep breath and blew into the valve again. The raft was almost fully inflated, but it had taken a really long time to get this far. First he'd had to calm Paul down. Then they'd had to dig the raft out from under all the rocks and dirt that had fallen on it. Luckily some of it had been poking out, and they had been able to get at it. At least George had been holding on to the piece of board when they'd run out of the room the skeleton had been in, so he still had his paddle.

Unfortunately, George hadn't been as lucky with his watch. One of the falling rocks must have hit the face of it, because the glass cover was cracked. The broken face looked like a spider's web. Even worse, the compass no longer worked. One of the coolest things about the watch had been the compass, which was a needle that floated in a small amount of water under the watch glass. But now that the watch was broken, the liquid had drained out and the compass was useless.

George had held the watch up to his ear and heard it ticking. At least it could still tell time. And the blue light still came on when George squeezed the buttons on both sides, but it didn't seem to glow as brightly as it had before it was broken.

Blowing up the raft hadn't been nearly as easy as George had hoped it would be. He felt like he'd been inflating it for over an hour now. His lungs hurt, and when he stopped, he saw little stars dance in front of his eyes.

Whooooooo!

That was the second time George had heard that sound. At first he had thought someone else was in the chamber with them. Then Paul told him what it was.

"That's the ghost wind," he said. "The big water is one thing I don't like down here. The ghost wind is the other."

George shivered. He gazed into the inky blackness of the lake chamber, where the sound seemed to come from. "There's . . . um . . . no such thing as ghosts," he said haltingly. "That's just . . . superstition. That's what my dad says. Nothing to be afraid of." George hoped he sounded more convincing than he felt. *Who are you trying to convince, anyway?* he thought. *Paul? Or yourself?*

Paul was pacing around behind him. George watched as he walked back and forth on the small piece of land between the pile from the rock slide and the underground lake. He nervously tugged on his right ear with his hand, and it looked like he was talking softly to himself. George stopped inflating the raft and continued to watch Paul out of the corner of his eye. He *was* talking to himself. *He's trying to psych himself up to do this,* George suddenly realized. *Wow.* That was pretty brave. George wasn't sure that he would be able to psych himself up to face his own two biggest fears—at the same time.

George had thought about asking Paul to help him blow up the raft but decided against it. *It's going to take every bit of courage he's got to get on this raft,* he thought. *I'd better not distract him.*

"It won't be so bad," George said between breaths. "See, when this raft is fully inflated, it floats on top of the big water. We'll be inside it, so we won't actually have to be *in* the water ourselves."

Paul was silent. Then he said, "What if it tips over?" George could hear the anxiety in his voice.

"It won't," George replied, trying to sound certain. "There won't be any waves down here, and I'll be sure to paddle really slow. We'll be fine. I promise."

But can I really make that promise? George thought. *That's a pretty big lake, and we can't see the end of it. Who knows what could happen to us out there?* But there was no point in being afraid of things you couldn't see. Well, except for the ghost wind.

Finally, the raft was fully inflated. "Okay, all finished," he said. George silently thanked Renee's parents for being such good campers. The raft was big enough to fit at least four people, and it looked pretty sturdy, too. It had a canvas shell on the outside, and it looked like it would take a lot to poke a hole in it. That made George feel better since he had no idea what lay under the surface of the water.

But as he dragged the raft over to the water's

edge, he could see fear mounting on Paul's face. He walked over to his friend and put a hand on his shoulder.

"I know you're scared. But we don't have any other choice. Even if we could dig our way through the rocks, it would take us weeks. We'd probably starve by then. The only way to get out of here is over the water."

Paul nodded, but he didn't speak. His face had a rigid set to it. He looked like he was trying really hard to stay in control and not look scared.

"Now, I need you to get in the front of the raft, Paul. Then I'll push it into the water and get in myself."

Paul stepped into the end of the raft. His footsteps were tentative, like he was afraid the raft would pop if he stepped in the wrong place. He made his way to the front and sat in the bow. There were plastic handles that were placed along the top of the raft. Paul held on to these so hard that his knuckles turned white.

"Okay, now I'm going to start pushing the raft into the water. Don't panic. Everything is going to be all right."

George pushed the raft slowly forward. The bottom scraped against the floor of the cave with a dry rasp. George hoped silently that he wouldn't drag it over a sharp rock and puncture it. But once the front end of the raft slipped into the dark water, the rest of the raft eased gently in.

George tried not to get his feet wet, but he wasn't entirely successful. Icy water seeped in through his sneakers and soaked his socks. *Oh, great,* he thought. *Soggy feet. What's next?* George hopped into the back of the raft, and it swayed from side to side.

"George!" Paul's eyes were wide with fear.

"It's okay, it's okay," George reassured him as the raft settled back to a level position. "We're fine."

The raft drifted away from the land and into the darkness. George dipped the flat end of the board into the water and paddled. The raft didn't move as much as he'd thought it would. George stroked again, and the raft moved a little bit more. He tried to get a steady rhythm going, and he did succeed in getting the raft to move a little faster through the water. But it was very slow going. This could take forever!

Paul was being very quiet, and George wasn't talking, trying to put as much effort as he could into his paddling. He was struck suddenly by how silent it was in the enormous chamber. It was like the dark surface of the water sucked in all the sound, like a black hole. But when there *was* a sound, like the drip of water from the ceiling into the lake, it echoed through the chamber, as if it were coming from all directions at once. Every little *drip* and *plop* made George's skin crawl, and he hoped they would be across the lake soon.

George tried to keep the raft toward the right-hand side of the lake. Or at least in the direction of where he thought the right side would be. According to the map, there was a tunnel on the southern shore, but it was to the right of where they had started. George hoped he'd be able to direct the raft somewhere close to that other shore. If he couldn't, they could be floating down here for a long time. With these creepy sounds. And the ghost wind.

George looked at the watch on his wrist. "Oh, no," he said, not realizing he'd spoken aloud. It was four-thirty. His stomach did a little flip. It was only a half hour before he was expected home, and he knew there was no way he was going to make it there that quickly.

"*Ohno . . . ohno . . . ohno . . .*" George started at the sound of his voice echoing throughout the chamber. He looked around cautiously, but there was nothing to see except the darkness and the water. He'd had no idea that their voices would carry that far once they were out on the water. The sound of his own voice echoing back at them was unnerving.

"What's wrong?" Paul looked back at George nervously.

"What? Oh, nothing's wrong with the raft. Don't worry."

"Then why did you say, 'Oh, no'?"

"I was just realizing how late it is. My dad is not going to be very happy when I get home."

"He doesn't know you're down here?" Paul asked.

"No. If he knew, he would never let me do this. He'd think it's too dangerous."

"He's right," Paul said, looking forlornly off into the dark. They still couldn't see where the lake ended, and they couldn't even see the tunnel where they'd pushed off anymore.

They were all alone, in the middle of an underground lake, in almost total darkness.

Whooooooo!

Ghost wind again. This time a chill went down George's spine.

For the first time it occurred to him how dangerous a situation this was. It was bad enough that he wasn't sure he'd be able to find his way out of the tunnels. But what made things even worse was that no one knew where he was! He had kept this little trip a secret from the others because he thought they might try to talk him out of it. As he dug the paddle into the water again and again, George started to wish they *had* talked him out of it.

George's fingers were beginning to hurt from the strain of paddling. The jagged end of the board he was using was making his hands raw and red. He had gotten more than a couple of splinters as well, and it was beginning to hurt just to hold the board in his hands. He stopped paddling for a moment to rest, but his hands hurt just as much when he started paddling again. What other choice did he have?

George paddled on for a while longer, trying to keep his pain to himself. Paul was very quiet in the front of the raft, and George didn't want to disturb his thoughts. So he tried to concentrate on all of the things he wanted to do once he got out of these caves, anything to take his mind off the pain in his hands. Some mint chocolate chip ice cream would be nice. With hot fudge, so the ice cream would melt and the flavors would run together. His stomach rumbled. He hadn't realized how hungry he was! He hadn't brought any food down with him, because he thought he'd be home in time for dinner. Even his dad's baked chicken would taste good right now. Heck, he wouldn't even turn down dinner in Little Litaria with Kira Trenov!

"Hey, what's that?"

Paul's voice snapped George out of his thoughts.

"What's *what*?"

"That." Paul pointed with his left hand. George followed the line of Paul's finger and saw something dark in front of them and off to the left. It looked like it might be solid ground. *But isn't that in the wrong direction?* he thought. He looked around. Now that they were out of sight of the shore, it was almost impossible to tell which direction they were going.

"Is that the other side?" Paul said. There was a note of excitement in his voice.

"I don't know." George pulled out the map with the lake on it. He didn't know what the scale of the map was, but he had gotten a feel for the distances they had traveled in the tunnels. As much as he wanted to believe they were all the way across the lake, he really didn't think they'd gone that far. Had they been going the wrong way all this time?

George's stomach dropped like a stone. He'd tried to keep them going in the direction of shore, but it was hard to navigate in the darkness. The light of his bright didn't carry very far. They could have been paddling in circles and they would never know it. They might even be heading back to where they had started from!

George knew he needed to make a decision— and fast, too. If that wasn't the shore up ahead,

then they would be wasting precious time by paddling over to it. But if it *was* and they went the
other way, they could be out here for a very long
time. He had to pick one of the two options.

"I think we should check it out," George said
finally. He hoped he sounded more decisive than
he felt.

He paddled on the right side of the raft only,
turning it to the left, in the direction of the shad-
owy bank ahead. It took a while to get there, but it
was definitely starting to look like land. George felt
a rush of relief. He couldn't wait to get off this lake!

"I don't think it's the other side," Paul said with
disappointment in his voice.

George stopped paddling and looked up. Paul
was right. It didn't look like the opposite shore.

"It's . . . it's an island," George said, amazed.
Who would have thought there would be an
underground lake under New York City, let alone
one big enough to have an island in it!

A little part of George wanted to land on the
island and check it out. But his common sense
talked him out of it. He was already majorly late,
and stopping here would just make him later. Plus
he was beginning to wonder if they were even going
to be able to find a way out. *That* was what was
really important now. Pirate stuff was beginning

not to feel as important anymore. But still . . .

George turned the boat back around and set off back in the opposite direction. But he couldn't stop himself from taking one look back at the mysterious island, wondering what secrets it might hold. As the raft moved slowly away, he thought he could see something on the surface of the island. He turned his bright toward it, and it slowly came into focus.

It was a tombstone.

A feeling like ice ran down George's back.

Whoooooo!

He started paddling faster.

George didn't speak for a long time after they paddled away from the island. The image of that lonely gray tombstone haunted him, and he wanted to get as *far* away from it as he could, as *quickly* as he could. He forgot the pain in his hands and gripped the piece of board hard as he drove it into the water, trying to propel them faster and faster with each stroke.

Eventually his pace slowed. He just couldn't keep it up anymore. The muscles in his shoulders burned, and his hands felt like they were on fire. George stopped paddling just for a moment to catch his breath and let his arms rest. That was when he noticed that the bright wasn't so bright anymore.

At first he thought it was just an optical illusion. But sure enough, he realized that the battery on his helmet lamp was running out. The light became dimmer and dimmer before them. Soon they couldn't see its reflection on the water anymore. It was just a dim, dull glow that barely lit up their faces in the small rubber raft. And then even that was gone.

When it first happened, George just sat in the raft, totally defeated. Not only were they cut off from the way they'd come, not only were they not sure that they were paddling in the right direction, now they had no light at all. The darkness pressed down on George.

Paul had kept saying that George and his friends didn't belong down here. Now George was starting to believe that Paul was right. But it wasn't just Paul; it was also Shannon, Derrick, and Renee. They had all thought it was too dangerous. If George hadn't been so stubborn, if he had only thought things through, he would have agreed with them, too.

Look at this situation, George thought. *I'm underground, in the middle of a lake. I think I know the right way to go, but I could be totally wrong. I may never get out of here. No one knows where I am. I may end up spending forever down here, just like Paul. And even if I do find a way out, my dad is going to ground me for the rest of my life!*

There's no question about it, he thought. *The others were right. If I'm lucky enough to get out of this mess, I'm going to quit, too. It's time for pyrate retirement. But the first thing I'm going to do is apologize for going off on my own without telling them. That's not something a good leader does.*

George pressed the buttons on the sides of his watch. Now it was almost six o'clock. Not that it mattered. They were so far away from getting out of the tunnels, it didn't make much difference what time it was.

Paul was watching George check his watch. "Are you still worried about your father? What's he going to do if he finds out?" Paul asked.

"Well, for starters, he'll probably ground me for a long, long time," George answered. It made him feel good to say that. If he thought about how much trouble he'd be in, it made it seem possible that he might make it home.

"What's that mean—'ground'?"

"It means I can't leave the house. Well, except to go to school. And I won't be able to go on the Internet—"

"In-ter-net?" Paul's eyebrows furrowed in confusion.

"Um . . . that one's kind of hard to explain. Basically, I won't be able to do a lot of things that are fun," George finished.

"I don't know," Paul said. "That doesn't sound too bad. My dad did worse things than stop me from having fun."

George thought about it for a moment. Paul had a point. It wasn't like he would have to go through anything like what Paul had gone through—escaping an abusive father by moving into subterranean tunnels. In the larger scheme of things, so what if he was going to get in trouble and maybe be grounded for a while? He still had a house and a father who cared about him. George looked at Paul, who was gazing out over the dark water. He felt a sudden sadness. He bet that Paul would be willing to be grounded forever in exchange for having a family.

"Your mom . . ." Paul began, hesitatingly. "She's gone . . . dead, like my mom, isn't she?"

"Yeah," George agreed. He had forgotten they had that in common.

"What was she like?" Paul asked.

George hesitated. He didn't know what to say first. "She liked to grow things. She had a garden behind our house, and she grew all kinds of flowers. Marigolds, tulips, snapdragons. Those were my favorite. Snapdragons."

Before he knew it, the words just started to come tumbling quickly out of George's mouth.

"She used to read to me every night before bed. We talked about pirates together, and she taught me the difference between a pirate and a privateer. She used to make me homemade macaroni and cheese every Thursday night because it was my favorite." George choked back a sob and felt a tear roll down his cheek in the dark. "And she used to call me her little prince."

George let the silent tears flow. Being in the dark didn't feel so bad all of a sudden.

"You really miss her," Paul said softly. "I know how that feels."

George cleared his throat. "What was your mom like?" he asked.

"She was tough," Paul said. "I don't remember a lot about the dayside. But I remember leaving. My dad was angry and yelling. And my mom yelled back. She said, 'You're not going to hit me or Paul ever again.'"

Paul paused for a moment. "Then we were here. She always said, 'Things will get better soon, Paul. This is just for now. We'll be better off before you know it.' She brought me food every night. 'Special supper,' she called it. I didn't know until after she was . . . gone . . . that she never ate the 'special supper.' She just brought it for me."

George realized what Paul was saying. His

mother spent all day finding enough food for Paul and then let him have it all, not eating any herself.

"Wow," George said. "Your mom sounds like she was really strong. Like she would have done anything for you. She must have loved you very much."

There was an awkward silence. George reached for something to say.

"I—"

"*Quiet!*" Paul hissed suddenly.

George hushed and ducked his head. What was going on?

"Look over there," Paul whispered, motioning toward the front of the raft. George lifted his head slightly and looked.

George didn't see it at first. But when he squinted, he could make out small lights dancing up ahead of them. His first instinct was to whoop for joy. Lights meant people, and people meant land. They'd done it! They'd made it to the other side!

But then George realized what else the lights might mean. People could mean Roulain and his thugs. They were the only other people down here who were likely to use lights.

"What do we do?" Paul whispered.

George thought about it, but there wasn't much choice. There was really only one thing to do.

"We're going to have to go toward them. It's our only way out of here."

George saw Paul's eyes narrow in the dark. He didn't seem to like this plan.

"It's either that or stay out here on the big water forever," George explained. "We'll just have to make a break for it when we land the raft. Maybe one of us will get away."

"I can outrun Leroy's men as long as there's not too many of them. They're slow," Paul said.

I hope you're right, George thought.

George started paddling again. His fingers were cramped from paddling for so long, and he had goose bumps all over his arms from the cold air of the chamber. *Just a little bit more,* he thought as he moved the raft in the direction of the lights.

As they got closer, George counted the lights. One. Two. Three. Three lights. That meant three men. George's heart sank. He didn't think they'd be able to get away from three men. But what choice did they have?

They were closing in on the opposite shore now. They could see a dark tunnel that opened out onto the lake. He also saw the silhouettes of the people with the lights. *Funny,* George thought. *We must be farther away than it feels. Those silhouettes still look pretty small.*

"Better stay low," Paul advised. "Don't let them see us until the last second. Then run for it. If the tunnels split, go right. I'll go left. Split them up. Our chances are better that way."

It was a good plan, better than any George could have come up with.

George stopped paddling and let the momentum carry the raft toward the shore. He readied himself by stooping into a crouch. He was ready to spring the moment the raft hit the shore.

But just before that happened, George heard a voice. A *familiar* voice.

"It's about time you got here."

Six

Gomes

George was shocked. That was *Shannon's* voice!

His head shot up in the back of the raft. As the little inflatable boat hit the shore with a gravelly *crunch*, George's eyes focused on the faces of Shannon, Derrick, and Renee.

What were *they* doing here?

Shannon reached out and grabbed Paul's hand, helping him safely to shore. Derrick gave George a hand out of the boat while Renee grabbed the side of the raft and made sure it didn't float away. George's hand was so sore from paddling that it was cramping up.

"What are you guys doing down here?" George asked.

"Well, I had to make sure you took care of my family's raft," Renee replied in a whisper. "My parents would be furious if anything happened to it!" She was grinning from ear to ear.

"We're here to rescue you, bonehead," Derrick said, giving him a friendly punch on the shoulder. "Next time you tell your dad you're coming over to my place, do me a favor and let *me* know about it, okay?"

George had completely forgotten that Derrick was his cover story. His dad must have called when he didn't get home on time.

"Was he mad?" George asked.

"Well, he was, until I explained that it was my fault for forgetting to call him."

"Huh?"

"I told him that my parents had invited you to stay for dinner and sleep over tonight. I said you were still playing football in the park with these guys"—he motioned toward Shannon and Renee—"and that I was supposed to call your dad and ask permission but I forgot. He was a lot less angry then," Derrick finished. "Then I rounded up Shannon and Renee, and we headed down here as fast as we could."

"How did you know where I'd be?" George asked. "I didn't tell anyone!"

Shannon rolled her eyes. "George, no offense, but you're not that hard to figure out. As soon as we knew you were missing, there was only one place you could be."

"I guess you won't be . . . grounded . . . now?" Paul asked.

"I guess not," George answered. His mind was racing as he tried to make sense of the situation.

"But . . . but why would you come back down here? I thought you guys quit."

They all looked at George like he was crazy. Then they all spoke at the same time:

"Never leave anyone behind!"

George was stunned. That was the last line of the oath he had made up right after he, Derrick, and Shannon had gone down into the tunnels for the first time.

"But . . . that's not even the *real* pirate oath, the one we found in Captain Kidd's journal. That's just the stupid one I made up."

"So what?" challenged Shannon. "We still took the oath, right?"

"Besides," added Derrick, "we had to do something. You were MIA."

"Yeah," Renee chimed in. "After all, the first part of Kidd's oath said to be true and loyal to the captain. And even though you're a fool for coming down on your own—you're still the captain."

George felt so grateful, he was afraid he might cry.

"How *did* you find us?" Paul asked.

"Well, it was no secret where you were going," said Renee. While she talked, she was letting the air out of the raft so they could fold it up again. "So we set out for the underground lake."

"I remembered the layout of the map," Derrick

said proudly. He tapped his temple with a finger. "Photographic memory, remember?"

"We followed the path that led to the lake, but then we came to a dead end," Shannon added.

"But it wasn't a real dead end," Renee said. "I could tell that the rocks and dirt had just fallen. And there was some dust in the air still."

"At first we thought the worst," Derrick said. "That you had triggered a booby trap and been buried alive."

"We almost *were*," Paul said. George shivered. He had forgotten how close that had come to actually happening. Then George and Paul told them the whole story of the skeleton with the suspicious rib.

"Whoa." Derrick shook his head in disbelief.

"So what did you guys do then?" George asked.

"We weren't sure *what* to do," Shannon admitted. "We knew that if you were buried under a ton of rocks and dirt, it would already be too late. But if you *weren't*, then we'd have to find another way to the lake."

"That's when I remembered something," Derrick spoke up. "We'd never explored the tunnel that branches off to the south from your house. We were going to check it out, but we got so caught up following Captain Kidd's clues that we never got around to it. I remembered that on the first map that tunnel leads off the bottom of the page. I figured it would eventually meet up with the other tunnels."

"Huh?" George was confused. "I think you lost me there."

"Here, get out the map and let me show you." Derrick laid the two maps side by side on the ground and turned his bright on them. Sure enough, there was a tunnel that continued off the bottom of the first map.

But Derrick was pointing to the second map now, which lay right next to the first one. "See how this tunnel continues on from the first map to the second?" Derrick traced his finger along the tunnel that George and Paul had taken to the underground lake. It crossed over the two maps.

George nodded.

"Well, look at *this* tunnel here." Derrick pointed to the lake on the map. At the south end of it was the beginning of another tunnel. Squinting at it, George realized that it was the one they were standing in at that moment. "See how it goes off to the south? I figured that's where the third map must go so the tunnel could continue."

George nodded slowly. He thought he could see where Derrick was going with this.

"So if the third map goes *here*"—Derrick pointed to the spot just under the second map— "then the fourth map must go *here*." This time he pointed to the space under the first map. "So the four maps together would make a perfect square, right?"

George was grinning from ear to ear. He couldn't believe that Derrick had figured this out with only two maps.

"So I figured that this tunnel must lead from the first map down to the fourth, and if that was true, then it probably also connected to the third map and then right to the lake. Voilà!"

George gave Derrick a high five. "You're a genius!"

"That's pretty smart," Paul agreed.

"Darn straight," Shannon confirmed. "No way would I have ever thought of that."

"How long did it take you to find the lake?" George asked.

Renee pressed the button on the side of her watch, and it lit up. "It's almost seven o'clock, and we got here just before you did, George. Jeez, it took us almost two hours to go the long way."

George let out a low whistle. "That's a long time."

"Yeah, and we had to use the Hudson Park entrance, because we wouldn't have been able to get into your house. So it was an even longer trip."

"But we were kind of held up along the way—" Shannon began.

"That's right!" exclaimed Renee, interrupting Shannon. "I almost forgot. On our way here in the new tunnels we walked through this really big chamber, and it was filled with crates. Hundreds and hundreds of crates."

"What was in them?" George asked.

"What wasn't!" Renee replied. "DVD players, iPods, computers, digital cameras—you name it. Any electronic device you can imagine."

"We think Roulain put them there," Derrick added. "That's why he's down here. Those have to be stolen goods, probably smuggled in from out of the country. And he's got the perfect place to hide them. What cop would ever come down here to look for them?"

George nodded thoughtfully. "That makes sense."

"Is that why he's trying to scare us out of the tunnels?" Paul asked. "He's stealing things and keeping them here?"

"It looks that way," George said. He was silent for a moment. Knowing that Roulain was more than just some kind of treasure hunter, knowing that he was actually a hard-core smuggler, made him seem that much more dangerous. George remembered what he had decided on the lake.

"Well, this would probably be a good time to tell you all that I think you're right," he said.

They all looked at him blankly.

"Right about what?" asked Shannon.

"About quitting. When I was out there on the lake, I had a lot of time to think. I realized you're all right. Roulain's going to get the diamond, anyway. It's too dangerous to try to claim a treasure that's already lost. I'm sorry you had to come all the way down here to find me, but this is definitely my last pyrate adventure."

George's friends all looked at one another as if they didn't know what to say. Finally, Shannon's face brightened. She laughed.

"Oh, well, that's fine if that's what you want, but *we're* not quitting!"

"Wha-a-at?" George couldn't believe his ears.

"There's something we still haven't told you. To get over into these tunnels, we had to sneak past Roulain's men," explained Shannon. "They were digging away with lots of crazy machines. It was like an excavation site."

"Yeah, I know," George said. "I saw them, too."

"The machines were making so much noise that it wasn't very hard to sneak by them. We could still hear them, even when we'd gone a long way past where they were," Shannon continued. "Then we heard a *really* loud noise."

"What was it?" George asked.

"We didn't know at first, but it came from the dig site. We snuck back to check it out, and when we got there, everything had gone crazy."

"It looked like something out of *The X-Files*," said Derrick, picking up the story. "Their lights were shining through a ton of dust. It was hard to see what was going on. But from listening to them all yelling at one another, we figured out that they had tripped one of Captain Kidd's booby traps!"

"What!" exclaimed George. "No way!"

"Yes, way!" continued Derrick. "From what we could tell, they dug down to a certain point and found a wooden box. But when they pulled on it, the floor beneath them started to give way. It was all they could do to keep from falling down into a deep pit."

"We didn't waste any more time once we figured out what had happened. We left them there and went back to trying to find you," Renee finished.

George looked at them all. The excitement was back in his friends' eyes, that was for sure. But did he dare believe what they were telling him?

"Don't you see what this means, George?" Shannon said. "You were right all along! You *can't* find the treasure without all four maps. Roulain is no better off than we are. In fact, he's worse off! Because *we* know how to think like pyrates!"

"So the treasure hunt is back on?" George asked.

"Yes!" they all shouted at once.

"All right!" George exclaimed. "Now how do we get out of here?"

They crept silently down the tunnel. At Paul's urging, they didn't have their brights on. It turned out to be a good thing, because if their helmet lights had been on, they might not have noticed the light up ahead until it was too late.

George stopped. He was careful to keep his voice low. "Was there a light in that direction when you guys came this way before?"

They all shook their heads.

"Uh-uh," Derrick confirmed in a whisper. "It was dark as night."

"But I think that's the tunnel where all the crates are," Shannon said. "It could be Roulain!"

"I'll sneak up and check it out," George said, turning in the direction of the light.

Paul caught his arm. "I'd better go, too," he said firmly. "I can move more quietly than you. Stay behind me."

George nodded and followed Paul down the

tunnel. Shannon, Renee, and Derrick sat in the dark and waited.

Paul crept down the tunnel as silently as a mouse. Even George couldn't hear him, and he was right behind him. George tried to mimic Paul's stealthiness. He didn't think he would ever be as good, but he thought he was doing pretty well.

Paul put up his hand, stopping George. Then he turned and whispered, "They're right ahead." Sure enough, George could hear muffled voices.

Paul pointed at a large rock that was about twenty feet ahead of them in the tunnel. "We're going to have to crawl over to that rock or else they'll see us. Stay low and no talking!"

George nodded and motioned for Paul to go. Paul got down on his belly and crawled slowly over to the rock. It felt like forever to George, but he knew it was best to be as careful as possible. When Paul was safely behind the rock, he waved George on. George got down on his stomach and slowly crawled over toward Paul. The dirt-and-rock surface of the tunnel floor scratched his belly and chest, even through his shirt. He tried to go as slowly as possible and not make a sound. Eventually, he crouched safely behind the rock next to Paul.

He could hear the voices more clearly now.

"I almost got collared by the cops last week."

The speaker sounded like he was bragging. His voice was scratchy and hoarse like dry sandpaper. It sounded harsh and dangerous and made George's skin crawl.

"Where were you?" This voice was higher, more excitable.

"Uptown, Broadway and Seventy-ninth Street."

"That's the Twenty-third Precinct. Good thing you didn't get grabbed. The cops in the Twenty-third don't let guys off easy. What were you doing up there, Gomes?"

Gomes must have been Sandpaper Voice's name. George snuck a look around the corner of the rock. He saw three men sitting around a small, crude campfire. One of them was holding a hot dog on the end of a stick over the fire. Another one was eating a cooked hot dog. George recognized him as Sam, one of the thugs who had captured Paul. George could see Paul tense with anger. He must have recognized Sam, too.

The other one was pacing back and forth in front of the other two. He had long hair that was dirty and tangled and looked like it hadn't been washed in a while. He also had a dirty beard that made him look dangerous. Even from a distance George thought his eyes looked wild.

The bearded man was speaking, and each raspy

word out of his mouth was like fingernails scraping on a chalkboard. George didn't think he'd ever forget that voice as long as he lived. "I was doing a job for some other guy—real easy, breaking and entering. I took some jewelry and a Discman, but I heard them waking up before I could get anything big."

The one with the hot dog on the stick spoke. He was the one with the high-pitched voice. "How did you almost get caught?"

"I was getting to that," Gomes said testily. "I got out of the building just as the cops were coming down the street. They actually stopped me and asked if I had seen anyone suspicious. Har!"

High Voice and Sam joined him in a laugh. "If you'd been doing a job for Leroy, you wouldn't have had to worry about being hassled by the cops."

George frowned. Did that mean Leroy was in with the police? Was there any way that the police could turn a blind eye to what Roulain was doing? It seemed impossible.

Sam spoke for the first time. His voice was deep and threatening. "You'd better not let Leroy know you're doing jobs for anyone else. He's the boss, and you know what he'll do if he finds out."

The other two men looked at him. George thought he saw fear in their eyes.

"In fact," Sam said, "if you know what's good

for you, you won't be pulling any more jobs for anyone else. Ever."

George turned to Paul. He had heard enough. Time to get back to the others.

"It was definitely Roulain's men," George told the others when they returned. "There were three of them, in the room with the crates. They were eating hot dogs, and it looked like they might be there awhile."

"Can we sneak past them, like we did last time?" Renee asked hopefully.

"I don't think so," George replied. "They're right in the middle of the room."

"Oh, man! What do we do now?" Shannon pounded her fist into her open palm.

George motioned them back down the tunnel until they were far enough away that they wouldn't need to worry about being overheard.

"Paul," George started. "Do you know any other ways out of here?"

Paul shook his head. "I've never been here before. And why would I want to go dayside?"

George chewed on his thumbnail nervously. He couldn't think of anything. He could almost feel the eyes of the others on him. He knew that they were looking to him, as the captain, to figure a way out. But sometimes being a good leader meant asking for help.

"Does anyone have any ideas?" he asked, looking around at all of them. "I'm fresh out."

"Did anyone see any other tunnels between here and the lake?" Shannon asked hopefully. But they all shook their heads.

"Let's look at the map again," Derrick suggested. "Maybe there's another one off the lake."

"Good idea," George said, unrolling the second map.

"Rats!" Shannon spat. "Only two tunnels: the one that's caved in and the one we're in now."

"Wait a minute," Renee said. "What's this?" She pointed to a skull and crossbones on the map. "There are two of them," she explained.

She was right. There were two skull-and-crossbones symbols in different parts of the map.

"Hmmm," George murmured. "What do you think it is?"

"Take out the first map for a minute," Renee urged. "I think this might be important."

George wasn't sure, but he didn't have any other ideas. He unrolled the first map, the one Derrick had re-created from his photographic memory after the original had accidentally been locked back in George's dad's desk in the attic.

"See—look!" Sure enough, there were two skulls and crossbones on this map as well, in positions similar to the ones on the second map. One of them was over the abandoned subway tunnel. The other was right in the middle of the square that represented George's house. "These all look the same. I don't think it's a coincidence."

"So what do you think they are?" George asked.

"One of them is right at your house," she replied. "So maybe Captain Kidd marked all the places where there were exits to the dayside."

George pondered this for a second.

"It would make sense that Kidd would want to have several places to get into and out of the tunnels," Derrick pointed out.

"Okay, let's say you're right," George conceded. "Let's take this entrance here." He pointed at the one nearest to where they were. "*That* entrance would be hundreds of years old. It's probably been built over with something by now, like a building or a road."

"Maybe," Shannon added. "But what do we have to lose? Our only other option is to wait until the goon squad moves on, and who knows how long that will take? We might as well explore in the meantime."

She was right. "Okay," George said. "This skull and crossbones is"—he looked around, orienting himself with the map—"*this* way."

They moved down the tunnel, back in the direction of the lake. They made it to the bend in the tunnel where the spot was on the map.

"Nothing!" Renee said, frustrated. "But I was so sure!"

"It was a good idea, anyway," George said. "Anyone got any others?"

"Wait, what's that?" Shannon was pointing over Derrick's head. Derrick turned around and turned on his bright. There was nothing, just the tunnel wall.

"Put the light higher," Shannon urged.

Derrick raised his head so the light would move up the wall. After a couple of feet it showed a hole in the wall, about ten feet off the floor.

"Aha!" Renee whooped. "I *knew* it!"

"But how are we going to get up there?" Derrick asked.

"One of us can get on another's shoulders and climb up," Renee suggested. "Then we can use the rope to pull each other up."

"Great!" Derrick said. "You can use my shoulders. Who's going to climb up first?"

"I think it should be me," Shannon said, stepping forward. "After all, I'm the heaviest."

They all looked at her, wide-eyed. She was pretty tall, but why would she think—?

"Trust me," she said.

"Hey, why should the heaviest one get on my shoulders?" Derrick asked, worried.

"Because if I'm going to help the next person up, I've got to be heavier than them or else they'll pull me right back down into the tunnel."

"Oh. Yeah," Derrick admitted. "I guess that makes sense."

George cupped his hands, and Shannon set her foot in them and let George boost her up onto Derrick's shoulders. Once there, Shannon crawled up into the hole in the wall. It was hard work. George could see her strain to pull herself up with her arms. She almost didn't make it, but at the last minute she heaved her legs over the edge and into the hole.

They could hear her breathing heavily in the dark. Then she said, "Okay, let's have the rope."

They threw it up, and Shannon tied one end of the rope around her waist and tossed the other end back down. Paul was the lightest, but Renee pointed out that she was the more experienced climber and would put less strain on Shannon. She tied the loose end around her own waist.

"Ready," Shannon called from the hole.

George cupped his hands again, and Renee climbed up on Derrick's shoulders.

"Okay!" Renee said to Shannon. Luckily, Renee was a seasoned rappeller, and she hopped up the wall in no time flat. Shannon really only needed to anchor the rope for her.

With two of them to pull on the other end, it was easier to bring the rest of them up. They went in order of weight, first Paul, who was lightest, then Derrick, then George. With four people pulling on the other end, they yanked George up in a hurry.

"It looks like there's a passage this way," Shannon said, pointing into the darkness. Sure enough, there was another tunnel. If they were lucky, it would lead out to the dayside.

They followed the tunnel for a while, and they could tell it was sloping upward. George was beginning to hope that it might actually get them out.

Derrick was out in front, his bright the only light. Up ahead a few yards George heard him say, "Whoaaa. . . ."

"What is it?"

The passage ended with a huge staircase that stretched upward and on into the darkness. The staircase was carved directly out of the stone of the tunnels. It was wet with moisture, and it was so steep, it looked like it went almost straight up. It looked really old. Old enough to have been built by Captain Kidd.

"How far up do you think that is?" Derrick asked, craning his neck.

"It's got to be over a hundred feet," Renee answered. If any of them could judge distances down in the tunnels, it was her.

"Well, no point just standing around," George said. "Let's start climbing."

The stairs were even steeper than they looked. It was hard going, too, because there were no handrails to hang on to. Once George turned around and looked back down. They were so high up and at such a steep angle, just looking down made George feel dizzy. He didn't turn around again.

It wasn't long before they were all huffing and puffing—even Paul. They rested every twenty steps or so before George urged them on again. It was getting late, and they didn't have time to waste, especially if these stairs led to a dead end. George kept that concern to himself. He didn't want to worry the rest of them.

The stairway eventually ended in a small landing, just big enough for the five of them to stand on. They caught their breath while Derrick flashed his light around.

"Nothing! I can't believe we climbed up all this way for nothing!"

"Wait," George said. "Let's not make the same mistake twice. Look *up*."

Derrick flashed his light up to the low ceiling,

which barely cleared their heads. "All right!"

Directly over their heads was a trapdoor. It looked almost exactly the same as the one in George's basement. The only difference was that it had a round handle, not an octagonal one.

"That's got to be it," Shannon said. She stepped aside and motioned to the trapdoor, like a maitre d' at a restaurant, looking at George. "Captain, after you."

George stepped up onto a ledge, then reached up and put his hand on the handle.

"Quiet, everyone," he warned. "The last time we tried a different exit to the tunnels, we ended up in Roulain's apartment. Who knows what we'll find up there?"

George grasped the handle and pushed.

Seven

GRAHAM HOUSE

At first the trapdoor wouldn't budge. It took George three tries before it moved at all, and even then it only moved a little bit. But it felt like George had loosened it.

"What's going on?" whispered Shannon impatiently. They were all tired and frustrated from being underground so long.

"It must have been a long time since this trapdoor was used," George replied, taking a moment to catch his breath before trying again. "I think the hinges are practically rusted shut."

George gave another shove, and a shower of dust fell over them as the door moved almost a whole inch.

"I can see light!" George called down, still keeping his voice low.

"That must be a good sign," Renee said hopefully.

George gave the door another shove, and this time it swung all the way open. There was a loud clatter. George cringed and lowered the trapdoor so he could only see a thin sliver of light. He waited, expecting the worst.

They were all silent for a few tense seconds. But if anybody was nearby, they didn't seem to have heard the noise.

"I think it's okay. I'm going to check it out," George said. "You guys stay here. And stay quiet!"

Slowly he raised the trapdoor again, lifting his head to peer over the edge.

It looked like he was in a kitchen decorated with very old furnishings. There was a simple wooden table in the center of the room, surrounded by equally simple chairs. All the furniture was stained very dark and had deep scars and cracks running through it. There were old-looking pots and pans made of black cast iron hanging on the wall and what looked like a butter churn in the corner. *Great,* George thought. *Whose apartment have I broken into now? Whoever it is, they really like the old-fashioned look!*

Then George saw something that made everything suddenly make sense. He lowered the trapdoor again and rejoined his friends.

"Well, where are we?" Derrick asked. He sounded a little impatient.

"I think it's a museum," George replied. "At first I thought it was the kitchen of a house that was just decorated in a really old style. But then I saw velvet ropes connected to those metal poles. This must be one of those old houses—you know, as old as mine—that's been turned into a historical monument or something."

"That's great!" Renee said with a sigh of relief. "We should be able to just pretend we're visiting the museum, and no one will know the difference."

"That's right," George agreed. "But we'll have to be careful. The trapdoor opens up into the fireplace in the kitchen. We've got to be sure no one walks into the room while we're climbing up, or we're going to scare some poor tourist!"

"What about you, Paul? Are you going to be able to find your way back?" Shannon asked, concerned.

Paul looked a little insulted. "Of course I can get back," he replied.

"What about Roulain's men?" Shannon pressed.

"I'll wait until they go. They won't stay there forever," was his response.

"You know, if you wanted to, I'm sure you could come with us and get back to the tunnels through George's house," Renee suggested.

"Yeah," said Derrick. "Who knows how long Roulain's thugs will be hanging around?"

But Paul shook his head emphatically. "Uh-uh. Don't want to go dayside."

"Are you sure?" Renee didn't seem to want to give up.

"Yes," he said firmly. "I don't belong up there. Down here I understand everything."

"Okay, if that's the way you want it," George agreed reluctantly. He paused and waited until his friends began climbing through the trapdoor. Then he took Paul aside.

"Paul, I just wanted you to know that I'm sorry we had to go over the big water. I told you that you wouldn't have to, and then we did. I know there wasn't much choice, but I'm sorry, anyway."

Paul gave George a funny look, like he didn't know how he should react. It seemed he wasn't only not used to people keeping promises; he wasn't used to people saying sorry, either.

"It's . . . okay," he said finally. "It wasn't so bad."

"You know, I never would have been able to get this far without your help. You're a good friend," he said. Then he added, "And a good pyrate."

George could see Paul's grin in the dark. "Thanks," said Paul.

"We'll try to come back tomorrow. Will you make it back to your tunnels by then?"

"Sure," Paul said as if it were the easiest thing in the world. Then he was gone.

George turned back to the others. One by one

they sneaked into the old kitchen. It felt like they had walked into another time period altogether. Everything was dimly lit, and the place didn't just look old, it *smelled* old. Luckily they all were able to climb out of the trapdoor without anyone walking in on them.

George saw something on the floor in the corner. He walked over and picked it up. It was a fake fireplace setup, a couple of logs nailed to a wire frame. It must have been sitting in the fireplace to look like a fire was about to be set. George guessed that was what had caused the sound they'd heard when he opened the trapdoor. George had shoved the trapdoor so hard, he'd knocked the fake fire halfway across the room! He put it back in its place and brushed the dust off his hands.

"Okay," he said. "Now let's get out of here."

"I think the exit is this way," Shannon said, pointing through a door on the left.

Sure enough, there was a sign hanging from the roof that read EXIT in letters that glowed red.

"Strange that we haven't seen anyone yet," Renee said, looking around. "This must not be a very popular museum."

"Do you know of *any* museums that are popular at dinnertime?" Derrick asked, and they all laughed. George laughed, too. He suddenly realized how good it felt to know they were safe aboveground.

"Oh, no," Shannon said suddenly.

"What's wrong?" George asked.

"That's why we haven't seen anyone," she said. "What time is it?"

George checked his watch. "It's seven forty-five."

"The museum's probably closed. That's why no one's here. And if it's closed, then . . ."

"Then we're locked in," Derrick finished.

"What's that! Who's there?" a voice called out from the darkness.

They froze in their steps.

The light from a flashlight bobbed across the floor toward them and then shone right in their eyes.

"Kids!" said a gruff, angry voice. "What're you kids doin' in here?"

George squinted. He couldn't quite make out the face of the man who was speaking to them because of the light shining in his eyes.

"Uh . . ."

"We got lost," Shannon piped up. "We were with a group from school, and we got separated."

"Lost?" They could tell by the tone of the man's voice that he didn't believe them. "A likely story! The museum closed forty-five minutes ago, and I checked all the rooms myself. Besides, what school takes a field trip on a Saturday?"

Shannon gulped. He had them there.

"You kids must've hid somewhere so you could get up to who knows what here after dark," the guard continued.

"But—"

Renee tucked the deflated raft behind her. George breathed a little sigh of relief—they didn't want this cranky security guard asking what they were doing with *that* in a museum.

"I don't want to hear your excuses!" the voice bellowed. The flashlight bobbed, motioning them past the guard toward what looked like the exit. "You better scat. And quick!"

They all rushed toward the door, not wanting to anger the guard any further.

"And don't come back, either!" he bellowed as they scampered out the door. "I'll recognize your faces, each and every one of ya! You'll never get back in this here museum as long as I'm workin' security!"

"Whew!" Shannon exclaimed once they were outside. "I thought he was going to throw that flashlight at us!"

"I can't believe we've been banned from some museum we never even knew existed," Derrick said.

As they stood around enjoying being in the fresh air of the evening at last, George saw a plaque on the side of the building. It read:

GRAHAM HOUSE

This house, built in 1683, was the original residence of Canton Graham, a prominent New York shipping magnate. Although Graham was an exporter of spices, he was also rumored to be tied to various smuggling and pirating operations. He was even linked to legendary pirate Captain Kidd. His house is now a historical monument, open to the public.

George realized Derrick was reading over his shoulder. "That would make sense," Derrick said. "If Graham knew Captain Kidd, then that would explain why he made an entrance to the tunnels through Graham's house."

"It's too bad," George said. "This place might have been useful in the future. But now we've been thrown out, and we didn't even get a chance to look around!"

Derrick nodded. "Yeah, that is too bad. I guess we might have found something important in there."

"Hey, you guys," Renee said. "We'd better get going, or all of our parents are going to be worried. I'm going to have a hard enough time sneaking this raft back into the house. It'll be even harder if I'm grounded!"

"You're right," George agreed. "Let's go."

*   *   *

Derrick and George sat in the back of a taxi-cab. They had just dropped Shannon and Renee off, and they were headed to Derrick's family's apartment. Derrick lived only a couple of blocks from George, but instead of in a house, he lived in a big apartment building. Derrick's family's apartment was on the seventeenth floor.

"My mom said she'd hold dinner until we got home," Derrick was saying. "Although it's after eight o'clock now, so she might be mad that we're home so late. So try to pretend that you like her dinner, okay? That'll help smooth things over."

"What is she making?"

"Meatless meat loaf," Derrick said with a groan.

"Oh, no!" George said suddenly.

"I know," Derrick replied. "It's pretty bad. But you have to pretend you like it—"

"No, not the meat loaf," George said. "I totally forgot. I went down into the tunnels through our basement, but I didn't come up that way."

"So what?" Derrick didn't see what the big deal was.

"So what if my dad goes down into the basement? The boxes are all moved around, and the hole in the wall that leads to the tunnels is in plain sight."

"Jeez! That's right!"

George noticed that the taxi driver's head was turned partway around, like he was listening to what they were saying. George looked at the name on his taxi license, which was posted on the Plexiglas partition that divided the backseat from the front. His name was Alexei Brantovski. *Great,* George thought. *With our luck he's probably Litarian, too.*

George lowered his voice. "We've got to go back so I can sneak into the basement and fix things in case my dad needs to go downstairs for something. If he hasn't already," he added. He wondered what he'd tell his dad if he really did discover their secret.

"Driver, we'll get out here," George said. It was a couple of blocks away yet, but he thought it would be better for them to walk than to have a taxicab pull up right outside his house. George got a twenty-dollar bill out of his pocket and paid the driver. As he took the change, he realized that he had spent almost all of his birthday money during the course of their pirate adventures. They'd *better* find the Eye of Eternity, or else he'd be broke!

George and Derrick sneaked up against the side of George's house. George was going to have to go in through the basement window. Luckily he had left it unlocked earlier, since he had planned on leaving the house to go to Derrick's, then circling back and letting himself in through the basement window. But since his dad and Kira Trenov had gone out, he hadn't needed to do that.

And it's a good thing, too, George thought. *Because if I had used the window, I probably would have locked it behind me. And then I'd really be stuck now!*

"Okay, Derrick, you keep watch while I sneak in," George instructed. "I'll try to be fast."

"Hey, who's that in there with your dad?" Derrick whispered suddenly.

The basement window was directly below the window to their kitchen. George peeked through the window. His dad looked like he was getting ready to cook dinner, putting pots and pans on the stove. But he wasn't alone. Kira Trenov was in the kitchen as well. They must not have gone to Little Litaria for dinner after all. Maybe they had decided not to after waiting so long for George to come home.

"That's the woman I told you about," George replied. "Kira Trenov."

"The Litarian scholar?"

"Yeah. *And* she claims some ancestor of hers was murdered by Captain Kidd. I don't trust her. What's she doing spending an entire day with Dad if she's not trying to get some information out of him?"

"Yeah, it does seem pretty suspicious," Derrick admitted.

George slid the basement window open as quietly as he could. He slipped in through the opening and lowered himself to the basement floor.

It didn't look like anyone had been down there, and the boxes were still pushed away from the wall. George quickly ducked into the hole in the wall and closed the trapdoor, making sure to latch it. Then he started moving the boxes back into their usual places. They were heavy, and George suddenly realized how tired he was. He'd been roaming around the tunnels, paddling on an underground lake, and climbing up and down ropes for hours! And now he had to push heavy boxes of books around.

George moved three boxes against the wall to cover up the hole. There were six boxes left, and George looked at them wearily. *Better hurry up or Derrick's parents will start wondering where—*

Suddenly, George heard a sound. It was the basement door!

George looked around wildly. He needed someplace to hide! He quickly ducked into a corner next to his dad's workbench.

The light snapped on, casting a shadow across where George was hiding. He pulled his knees up to his chin so his shoes wouldn't show.

"Let me just get a can of peas," he heard his dad say, and George heard footsteps descending the stairs.

George's heart was pounding in his chest. He

listened as his father opened the pantry under the stairs. His dad whistled cheerily as he rooted around the canned goods stored there.

When George heard the sound of the pantry door closing, he thought he might be in the clear. His father might not even notice the boxes! George couldn't believe his luck. But then . . .

"What the heck?"

Uh-oh.

"What is it?" It was Kira Trenov's voice, coming down the stairs from the kitchen.

"It's just George again," his father replied, and George winced at the tone of disappointment in his voice. "He's moved all the boxes around down here. He must have been looking for a book, but he never bothered to straighten up when he was done. After he just spent all that time cleaning the basement, too. I honestly don't know what's gotten into him lately. First he doesn't tell us about his plans with Derrick and we find out so late that we can't go to Little Litaria, and now *this*."

"Oh, Peter, boys will be boys," Kira Trenov said. George hoped she wouldn't come down the stairs. He didn't want her seeing the boxes of books and getting any ideas about what might be hidden behind them.

"Maybe," his father said. "But when he gets

back from Derrick's tomorrow, he's going to clean up this basement again. And then I've got a few more chores for him as well."

George swallowed in his hiding place. So much for going back to the tunnels tomorrow!

He heard the sound of his father's footsteps going back up the stairs, and then the basement was plunged into darkness as the light was turned off. The door closed.

George let out his breath. That was close!

He waited a few moments for his eyes to readjust to the darkness, then made his way back toward the window. At least he wouldn't have to move the rest of the boxes now that his dad had already seen them. He had all day Sunday to do that.

Once he and Derrick were away from the house, he filled his friend in on what had happened.

"Wow," Derrick said. "It's a good thing you got back when you did. A couple minutes more and your dad would have seen the whole thing!"

"Yeah, but now I've got to do chores all day tomorrow. We won't be able to go back into the tunnels."

"Oh, yeah. Well, at least we *can* go back, thanks to you."

George was silent for a moment. "Actually, thanks to all of us," he said. "Especially you. If you hadn't gotten everyone together, I'd still be down there with Paul. My dad would have found the trapdoor in the basement, and the whole adventure would have been over. I owe you big time, buddy."

Derrick looked embarrassed. "Well, if you owe me big time," he said, breaking out into a smile, "then you're *really* going to have to pretend that you like my mom's meatless meat loaf!"

Eight

OPERATION: MAPSNATCH

At school on Monday, George felt sorer than he ever had in his life. He had thought he was sore on Sunday morning after he woke up aching at Derrick's apartment. But that was before his father had him move the boxes back into place in the basement and then move a bunch more boxes into the attic for storage. His arms felt like he was dragging two-ton weights with each hand.

"Hey, George."

George turned and saw that Shannon had gotten into the lunch line behind him. They were in the cafeteria, getting ready to meet with the others.

"What are you having today?" she asked. "Baked ziti or the chicken surprise?"

"Last time I had the baked ziti, I had a stomachache for a week," he admitted. "But then again, I don't know if I'm up for a surprise." He still wasn't sure what had been in Derrick's mom's "meatless meat loaf." That had been enough of a surprise for him—especially the fact that it hadn't tasted half bad.

"Baked ziti," George mumbled to the lunch lady when it was his turn. He watched as the lunch lady slopped a scoopful of soggy noodles and sauce on his tray.

"Chicken surprise," Shannon said cheerfully. Didn't anything get her down?

They walked over to the table in the back where they held their lunchtime meetings. Derrick and Renee were already there. They had also taken the chicken surprise. George was beginning to wonder whether he'd made the wrong choice.

"So," he said, getting down to business right away. "Now that we're all back in the gang, what's our next step?" He had an idea of his own, but he wanted to see what the rest of the group thought. Part of being a good captain was listening to your crew, after all.

"I think we need to find the third map," Derrick said immediately. Renee and Shannon nodded in agreement.

"So do I," George agreed. "But where is it?"

"What about that island you saw on the lake?" Renee asked. "You didn't look there."

"Yeah," Shannon said. "Didn't you say there was some kind of tombstone?"

George shivered, remembering how spooky it had looked in the darkness. He nodded.

"Well, maybe *that's* where the skeleton is. The one whose chest has the third piece of the map."

"That's makes sense," George agreed.

"But it will take forever to get back to the lake going the long way," Renee reminded them. "There's no way we could make it there and back while your dad is playing bridge with the St. Johns on Tuesday night."

"That's true," George had to admit. "So we'll have to wait until Saturday." It was only five days away, but it seemed like a lifetime.

"You know," Shannon said suddenly, "I've been thinking. What good does it do for us to find the third map when we know we're not going to be able to get the fourth one?"

They were all silent for a moment. No one had thought that far ahead.

"Roulain's got the fourth map," Shannon continued. "And even if he can't find the treasure with just the one map, *we* can't find the treasure if we only have the other three."

"Jeez," Derrick said. "That's right. And there's no way we can get ahold of number four."

"Well . . . ," Shannon began. "I'm not sure that's true. We know he's got the map, but we also know how to get into his apartment."

"What are you saying?" Renee asked, looking

shocked. "You don't think we should steal the map from Roulain, do you?"

"No way!" Derrick exclaimed. "He'll know it's us for sure. And he's a dangerous guy."

"Yeah," George agreed. "I don't know why he hasn't tried anything on us yet, but if he knew we'd stolen his map, there's no telling what he'd do."

"Well, we'll just have to keep him from knowing that we have it."

They all looked at Shannon in confusion.

"How are we supposed to do that?" Derrick demanded.

"Well, not *we*," she replied, looking straight at Derrick. *"You."*

"Me?"

"You're always bragging about your photographic memory," Shannon went on. "This is the perfect use for it. You sneak into Roulain's apartment when he's not there, find the map, look at it, and get out before he comes back. Then you can just redraw the map from memory, like you did with the first one."

Derrick looked like he'd swallowed a bug. "Why did I even ask?"

George was intrigued but not quite convinced. "How are we supposed to know when Roulain will be gone from his apartment long enough to do it?" he asked Shannon.

"Well," she replied with a grin, "I've got a plan. . . ."

George had never eaten one of his father's meals so quickly. He was nervous about Operation: Mapsnatch and eager to get supper over with and his father over to the St. Johns' for bridge. But he hadn't counted on Kira Trenov joining them for another meal.

"Kira will be playing cards with us tonight," his father had said, gazing at Professor Trenov with a grin. "So we might be a little later than usual, around ten-thirty. At least, we will be if she's as good at bridge as she tells me she is." His father and Professor Trenov shared a smile. "I might even beat the St. Johns for once. Wouldn't that be something!"

"Sure would!" George said with as much enthusiasm as he could muster.

"What will you and your friends be up to this evening, George?" Professor Trenov inquired.

George tried not to look as suspicious as he felt. *I'll bet she'd like to know what we're going to be up to.*

"Nothing much," he said. "Just playing video games and stuff." He blushed. He wished he could have come up with a more convincing cover story.

"Just make sure you don't make a mess, like you did in the basement on Saturday. What were you looking for down there, anyway?"

"Um . . ." George's mind raced to come up with an answer. "I was just looking for . . . a book on Litaria," he mumbled. "I thought maybe I could find something on that Litarian duke that Professor Trenov was talking about the other day."

"Hmmm. You won't find anything on him in any of my books, I'm afraid," his father said. "I'd never even heard that legend until Kira told me. I've read all of those books downstairs cover to cover. I would have remembered something like that."

"Oh," George said, pretending to be disappointed.

"But if you are so interested in Litarian history, you should have come with us to the museum," Professor Trenov said. "It was very interesting. Wouldn't you agree, Peter?"

There she was, using his father's first name again. *I bet it was interesting. I bet you tried to find out what my dad knows about the tunnels and the maps. Unluckily for you, he doesn't know anything about them. And you're not getting any information out of* me.

"Oh, yes," his father responded brightly, smiling at Professor Trenov. "It was a fascinating exhibit. We really must take you there, George, before the exhibit closes."

"Yeah, I guess so," George said, not wanting at all

to see an exhibit full of moldy old Litarian artifacts.

"Oh! Look at the time," his father said, glancing at his watch. "We'd better get going, Kira. We can't beat the St. Johns at bridge if we never arrive, can we? George, please clear the table before your friends come over."

"No problem!" George replied, eager to get them moving. "Have a good time!"

Everyone was in place. It was time to put Operation: Mapsnatch in motion.

"Kidd to crew. Kidd to crew. Everyone report in," George said into his walkie-talkie. Shannon had insisted that they make up radio names for one another and that they all be pirate names. George was "Kidd" because he was their captain.

"Jolly Roger to Kidd." Shannon's voice came through the walkie-talkie. "I'm in place."

"Roger that, Jolly Roger." George wished he hadn't let Shannon use the name "Jolly Roger." "Roger" was what you said over a walkie-talkie to mean "okay." This could get confusing!

"Skull and Crossbones are in place," Renee reported. She had picked "Skull," leaving "Crossbones" for Derrick.

"Roger, Skull and Crossbones. Hold your positions and wait for my signal. Over."

"Are you talking to me?" Shannon said.

"No, Jolly Roger," George radioed back. "I was just saying, 'Roger.'"

"Oh," Shannon called back. "Roger."

George picked up the phone in his father's bedroom. Before he dialed the number, he held up the pair of binoculars he was holding in his left hand. He looked out of the bedroom window at the building two doors down. Two floors up and three windows over, George could see the windows of Roulain's apartment. Roulain himself was walking back and forth between rooms, getting papers from filing cabinets and working at his computer. *Probably counting all his stolen money,* George thought grimly.

He dialed Roulain's number with a shaky finger. His palm was sweating nervously where he held the receiver to his ear. He knew that all of his friends were counting on him. He just hoped that his talent was as reliable as everyone else seemed to think it was.

The phone rang once. Twice. Three times.

"Hello?"

George took a deep breath. He tried his best to summon the image of Roulain's henchman in his mind and silently hoped that his voice-mimicking skills were up to the challenge. He'd practiced the

henchman's voice so often that afternoon in prepa-
ration, he didn't even know if it sounded like that
of the nasty-looking thug he'd seen in the tunnels.

"Boss, it's me, Gomes," George said. George
rasped his voice, just like the sandpaper voice of
Gomes. It made the back of his throat hurt.

"You idiot!" Roulain screamed into the phone.
"I told you never to call me here!"

This outburst took George off guard. He
thought about just hanging up the phone. But
there was too much at stake.

"I know, boss. I know," George went on. "But I've
been collared by the cops. I'm at the Twenty-third
Precinct uptown. I need you to bail me out." George
tried to use words that he'd heard Gomes himself
use, like *collared*, so it would sound more genuine.

"Oh, for—" Roulain cut himself off. He
sounded almost too angry for words. "And why
should I bother to bail you out? I should let you
rot in jail."

George was prepared for this. He hoped he
could make it sound convincing, but the fact that
Roulain seemed to believe it was Gomes made
him more confident.

"Well, boss, I know an awful lot about that tunnel operation of yours. It would be a shame if the
cops found out about it. A *real* shame."

There was silence on the other end of the phone. For a panicked second George was sure that Roulain had seen through his deception.

"Fine. I'll be right there." Roulain slammed down the phone.

George couldn't believe his luck. It had worked! He wished someone were there with him to high-five.

He turned on his walkie-talkie instead.

"Jolly Roger, Roulain's on his way down. Let us know when he goes past. Crossbones, get ready to move. Over."

George watched through the window as Roulain angrily grabbed a coat and dashed out of his apartment, slamming the door.

A few minutes later he heard Shannon's voice come over the walkie-talkie. "The chicken has flown the coop. Repeat, the chicken has flown the coop. Over."

George smiled to himself. Shannon was really getting into the whole spy game, and she was good at it, too. After all, Operation: Mapsnatch had been *her* idea.

Shannon was waiting in the alley outside Roulain's apartment. It was lucky that Roulain's apartment was so near—the walkie-talkies would be in range. Her message meant that Roulain had left the building on his way to bail out Gomes. Wouldn't Roulain be surprised when he got to the Twenty-third Precinct and found no one there!

George pressed the talk button on his walkie-talkie. "Crossbones, you're up. Skull, keep a sharp lookout. Over." Derrick and Renee were down in the tunnel by the elevator that led to Roulain's apartment. Renee was to keep watch on the tunnels while Derrick went upstairs.

The seconds seemed like hours while George sat in his father's bedroom. He had left the lights off so he could see Roulain's apartment better. As it was, he could only make out whatever was right in front of the window. *Come on, Derrick,* he thought. *We've got to be quick!*

Finally, through the window, he saw Derrick appear in Roulain's apartment. He was in!

George watched as Derrick quickly rummaged through the papers on Roulain's desk. He didn't seem to be finding anything.

"Crossbones, try the file cabinet, the big black one to the side of the desk. Over," George radioed to Derrick. Derrick went over to the file cabinet George had seen Roulain using just minutes before. He leafed through file after file, drawer after drawer. George was getting more nervous as the minutes ticked by.

"Hurry up," George whispered to himself. Then he saw Derrick's head pop up. He had a big smile. He gave George a thumbs-up sign and showed the map in his other hand.

"All right!" George shouted into the walkie-talkie. "Now just memorize it and get out of there!" He'd almost completely forgotten the walkie-talkie speak. "Um, over," he added hastily.

Another voice broke through on the walkie-talkie. It was Shannon.

"He's coming back! Roulain's coming back! Derrick, get out of there!"

George was stunned. Roulain couldn't possibly have gotten uptown and back that fast. He must have forgotten something. Maybe the money for Gomes's bail.

"Get out, Derrick," George advised. They had completely dropped their code names. "Take the elevator back down to the tunnels and hurry!"

Then another voice came over the walkie-talkie. This time it was Renee.

"Don't call the elevator, Derrick! Two of Roulain's men just got in it, and they're going up to the apartment right now!"

Oh, no! George froze in horror. What was Derrick going to do? Roulain was coming up through the normal building entrance, and his men were coming up through the tunnel elevator. Derrick was trapped! Thoughts raced through George's mind like lightning.

"Hide!" he screamed into the walkie-talkie. "Find someplace to hide in the apartment right now! They'll be there any moment."

George's eyes were riveted on Roulain's window, and he saw Derrick disappear from his line of sight. Hopefully he had found a good hiding place. Then George had a thought. "Radio silence, everyone. Nobody say a word until I give the go-ahead. If anyone uses the walkie-talkie while Derrick's in the apartment, it will give him away!" George placed his walkie-talkie on his father's bed so he wouldn't press the talk button accidentally.

George watched the empty windows of Roulain's apartment, wishing he could see more. Then he saw Roulain. He sure hoped Derrick was well hidden!

George shifted nervously from foot to foot, watching Roulain root through his desk. Then George saw two other men appear over Roulain's shoulder—and one of them was Gomes! Oh, no! Their plan was blown for good.

Bzzzzt!

George almost jumped straight up in the air. What was *that*?

Bzzzzt!

It was their front door buzzer. Someone was at the door! But who?

George moved toward the bedroom door, then jerked back toward the window. What should he do? He didn't want to leave the window in case something happened to Derrick. But if he didn't answer the door . . . What if it was his father, locked out? Or some other kind of emergency?

Bzzzzt!

George threw up his hands in frustration and ran quickly down the stairs. He yanked open the door.

"Oh!"

It was Mrs. St. John, from next door.

"You surprised me, George, whipping the door open like that," she said, her hand at her throat in surprise. "I certainly hope I wasn't interrupting anything."

"Oh . . . no, not really," George said quickly.

"Well, where are all of your friends? I thought your whole crew was over here tonight. Not up to anything dangerous, I hope?" she asked with a mischievous, knowing wink.

"They're . . . upstairs. In my room. Playing video games." George hoped that sounded authentic.

"I'm just over for some sugar for our tea," Mrs.

St. John said, walking past him into the living room and heading for the kitchen. "I can't believe we ran out! I was certain I had bought some the other day, but I can't find it anywhere. Sometimes I think I'd lose my head if it weren't attached."

"Sugar's in here!" George said, directing Mrs. St. John into the kitchen and trying to speed things up. He hopped up on the step stool and pulled the container down off the top shelf.

"Are you enjoying the book we gave you for your birthday?" Mrs. St. John asked. She definitely wasn't picking up on George's attempts to hurry her along as she slowly spooned the sugar into the jar she'd brought with painful precision. George didn't think it was possible for her to spoon any slower. He felt like he was ready to jump out of his skin.

"Um, I'm enjoying it lots," he mumbled, wishing he had the time for a more genuine "thank you." George's father had mentioned once that the St. Johns hadn't been able to have kids. George thought that maybe she liked spending time with him because she wished she had a child of her own. George really liked Mrs. St. John, but at that moment he wished she would just hurry up and leave.

"Oh, I'm so glad!" Mrs. St. John said brightly, fitting the top back on the container and handing it back to George. She paused. "I must say, we're enjoying the company of Professor Trenov so *very* much. Don't you?"

"Oh . . . yeah, Professor Trenov's great," George lied.

"So odd how she just popped up one day, almost out of nowhere. How lucky for your father."

Lucky? George thought. Why would that be lucky for his father? If anything, it was unlucky— for all of them, if his suspicions about her were right.

But George didn't have time for all of that. He had to get back upstairs.

"Yeah, sure is strange. Funny world, huh?" he said, giving Mrs. St. John a nudge through the door.

"Oh!" she exclaimed, looking surprised. "Yes, well, I guess I'd best be getting back to our game and letting you get back to yours. Be seeing you!"

"Bye!" George called after Mrs. St. John. He shut the door as quickly as possible and turned and bounded up the steps, taking two at a time. He dashed into his father's room.

George ran to the window, and his heart sank in his chest. Roulain's apartment was now pitch-black.

What had happened to Derrick?

Nine

UNJUSTLY KILLED

George wanted to scream in frustration. Something had happened while he was downstairs talking to Mrs. St. John. But what?

Had Roulain and his men discovered Derrick? Had they imprisoned Derrick, like they'd imprisoned himself and Shannon?

George reached instinctively for his walkie-talkie. He was about to press the talk button when another thought struck him: What if Roulain was still in the apartment? It was dark, and George couldn't see him, so he assumed he wasn't there. But what if he was? George would be giving Derrick away for sure!

There was a sudden burst of static from the walkie-talkie. George barely stifled a scream and almost dropped it, he was so surprised.

"Come in, everyone," said Renee's voice. What was she doing? Hadn't George ordered radio silence?

"Roulain and the other men just stepped out of the

elevator and went off into the tunnels. Crossbones, you'd better get out of there now!"

George heaved a huge sigh of relief. Derrick was fine . . . for now. Renee had even waited until the coast was clear before breaking radio silence. Thank goodness.

"Better not use the elevator, Crossbones," George instructed. "Go out through Roulain's front door and come right back over to my house."

"Roger," Derrick replied. "Let me just put the map back so Roulain doesn't suspect anything."

"Skull," George called into the walkie-talkie. "You'd better get back up here fast. You don't know how long they'll be down there. They could come back at any time. I'll go down to the basement and help you up."

"Roger," Renee radioed.

"What?" Shannon responded. "Are you talking to me?"

"Jolly Roger, wait outside until Crossbones comes out of the building and then come back here with him."

"Roger," she replied.

George hurried down to the basement to help Renee.

*   *   *

By the time Shannon and Derrick returned, Renee had climbed back up the shaft, and she and George had covered up the hole with the boxes.

George was dying to know what had happened. So were Renee and Shannon. George had forgotten that they couldn't even see into Roulain's apartment—they could only tell what was going on by what they heard over the walkie-talkies.

"I couldn't see much from under the bed," Derrick said. So *that's* where he had hidden! "But Roulain yanked the door open so hard, I thought it was going to pull right off its hinges! He started rustling through the papers on his desk like he was looking for something—and in a hurry!

"Then the next thing I know, I hear the elevator doors open. Out stepped these two guys, and one of them was Gomes. I couldn't get a good look, but I would've paid a million dollars to see the expression on Roulain's face! He screamed at Gomes, calling him irresponsible and saying that he was messing up the whole operation. It took him a while to figure out that it wasn't Gomes who had called him from the Twenty-third Precinct. That's when he said, 'I'm going to get to the bottom of this!' and they left in the elevator."

They all shook their heads in disbelief. It was

terrifying to think how close Derrick had come to getting found out.

"Did you get a good look at the map?" George asked anxiously.

"I did," Derrick replied. "And you are not going to believe this. If you thought the other clues were hard, this one's going to make your heads spin. It goes—"

Honk!

They all flinched. Then they realized what the sound had been. It was Shannon's mom, come to pick them up.

"Ugh," Derrick said. "I guess we'll have to wait until tomorrow!"

George watched his friends leave, wishing Derrick had had just a couple more minutes to tell them what the fourth clue was. Now they'd have to wait until tomorrow. George was so nervous and excited that he paced back and forth in the living room until his father came home.

"George, didn't I ask you to clear the table?"

George thumped the heel of his palm against his forehead. With all the excitement of Operation Mapsnatch, he had completely forgotten.

His father frowned. "I don't know what's gotten into you lately. Your mind seems to be someplace else completely. Is something wrong at school?"

George shrugged. "Nah, everything's okay at school,

Dad. I guess I just forgot. Sorry." He walked over to the kitchen table and helped his dad pick up the plates and silverware. His father turned on the faucet in the sink and stopped up the drain. They would have to soak the dishes in the sink because they'd been sitting out dirty for so long.

George's dad looked at him with concern. Then he just shook his head, dismissing whatever it was he had been about to say.

"You know, George," he said suddenly, "I would appreciate it if you were nicer to Professor Trenov. She's a valued colleague, and she's becoming a close friend."

George felt himself burn. He wanted to say something, just blurt it out: *She's not a colleague* or *a friend! She's some kind of spy or treasure hunter, and she's up to no good, and I'm going to prove it to you!* But he didn't have any proof. At least, not yet.

How could he get proof against the mysterious Professor Trenov? Well, she was supposed to be a professor from Oxford University in England. George made a mental note to check the Oxford web site from the computer lab at school the next day. They must list their faculty on their web site, and George had a sneaking suspicion that Kira Trenov's name would *not* be on the list.

"Okay, Dad," said George finally. "I'll try to be nicer to her."

The next day at school, the gang met in the auditorium again. Derrick had brought in his version of the fourth map, redrawn from memory. They all crowded around him to look at it.

"That clue is, like, way longer than the others." Shannon pointed to the writing in a corner of the map. "Probably means it's way *harder*, too."

They all read it silently to themselves:

> Twenty stout men a good pyrate crewe be
> Forty arms, for sails to haul
> Forty eyes, to watch for all
> But 'tis their feet ye will sorely need
> To go from the mast's base to its peak
> If the true meaning of my treasure ye seek

At first nobody said anything.

"Are you sure you remembered that right?" Shannon asked, looking at Derrick. "It doesn't make a lot of sense."

Derrick looked at her, his pride a little hurt. "Erosion," he reminded her. George laughed to himself. When Shannon had first tested Derrick's photographic memory, she had tried to trick him into thinking he'd copied the word *erosion* wrong from a page of a science textbook. But he hadn't. He had passed the test with flying colors.

Shannon blushed. "Oh, right. Sorry."

"I don't get this part about a *mast*," Renee said. "There's no room for a mast down there. The ceilings are too low."

"You know," Derrick spoke up, "when we snuck by Roulain's men on Saturday, there was an old decayed log sticking out of the ground a little way past where they were digging. It had to be about fifteen feet long. Do you think that might be part of a mast?"

George thought about it for a moment. "Yeah, that could be. It would explain why they were digging there. But if that's the *wrong* place, it doesn't help us find the *right* one."

"What I can't figure out is *that* part," Derrick said, pointing to the last line. "What does he mean, 'the true meaning of my treasure'? We know what the treasure *is*—it's the Eye of Eternity. But what is its *meaning*?"

They all shook their heads. "I never thought of treasure having a meaning," Shannon said. "I just thought it was, you know, *treasure*."

Everyone was quiet for a while, trying to figure out the riddle. George could see that everyone was getting discouraged. "You know, I don't think it's such a big deal for us to figure this out right now," he said. "I mean, we don't want to make the same mistake Roulain did, so we shouldn't even think about solving this clue until we have the third map, too. Maybe that will help us solve it."

They all nodded in agreement. No one seemed to mind putting off trying to solve the riddle. It was kind of like a teacher telling them they wouldn't have to take a test until later in the week.

"We should plan our next move," George continued. "We've got to find the third map. It's the missing link."

Shannon nodded vigorously. "Right on, Cap'n. Any ideas?"

"Unfortunately, yes. I think you and Renee are right and the third map is on the island in the underground lake. I saw a tombstone on that island, and right now that's the only dead guy we know about down there."

"Oh, man!" Derrick moaned. "I am so sick of skeletons! I suppose we're going to have to dig this one up?"

George sighed. "I don't see any other way."

They were all quiet for a moment. None of them seemed particularly pleased at the prospect of digging up a corpse.

Finally, Renee spoke. "We've got some collapsible shovels with our camping gear. The handles fold down so they're easier to carry."

"Great," George said. "And we'll need the raft again."

"Okay," Renee said. "But someone's going to have to help me clean it off afterward. It got a lot of mud on it last time, and I don't want my parents asking questions. They always leave it clean as a whistle."

"Hey, I just noticed something," Derrick said, looking at the map. "I remembered this last night but totally forgot it until just now. Look at the skulls and crossbones."

"You mean the exits?" George asked.

"Yeah, the little symbols that mark the exits. Look," he said, placing the fourth map in position with the first two. "There are two on each map."

"Okay, so?" Shannon asked, puzzled.

"It's not just that there's two on each map," Derrick went on. "They're all kind of in the same position on each map." He drew his finger across the three maps in an arc. "It's three quarters of a circle."

"Hey, you're right," Renee said.

"I bet when we find the fourth piece, it'll have two *more* skulls and crossbones, and then we'll have a complete circle," Derrick finished.

"But what does it mean?" Shannon asked. "Why would Kidd put all of his exits in a pattern like that?"

But before they could puzzle it out any further, the bell rang. They all had to get to their next classes. George carefully packed up the maps and said, "Okay, everyone think about the clue and why the exits are in a circle. We'll go down to the tunnels on Saturday and head for the lake!"

For once, George was in luck. His father was going on a day trip to Long Island that Saturday afternoon. George wasn't happy that the person he was going on this trip with was Kira Trenov, but he figured that if she was way out there, then at least she wouldn't be snooping around their house. And because his dad was going to be gone for most of the day, George didn't have to make up any lies or sneak his friends into the basement.

Renee had smuggled each piece of equipment they'd need into school: the raft one day, the shovels the day after that. Each day George had hidden the equipment outside the basement window and then snuck down to the basement later in the night and brought it inside. By Saturday they had everything they needed.

Another stroke of good luck: Roulain's men were back to digging, but they were digging in a completely different section of the tunnels, closer to where the shantytown had been before Roulain scared all the homeless people away. George couldn't figure out why Roulain had chosen that particular spot, but he was relieved because it meant they wouldn't have to sneak directly past them to go to the lake. George's gang was as alert as they could be and only went down each tunnel one at a time, with the first person checking before waving the next along. They didn't talk at all and rarely used their brights. They were so good, in fact, that when Paul sneaked up on them, none of them screamed in surprise. They just motioned him on with them, as if he'd been there all along.

On the way toward the lake Derrick noticed a branch of the tunnel they hadn't remembered seeing when going back in the other direction. It was before they reached the exit to Graham House. It branched off to their left. George wanted to check it out.

"I just want to see if it leads to anything," he said. "I'll be right back."

He padded softly down the tunnel, shining his bright on the path in front of him. About twenty-five feet in, he felt the air change. It was a little colder. He'd definitely walked into a larger room.

He shone his bright against the wall.

It was like the section of tunnel that Roulain had used to store his smuggled electronics goods. But this time it wasn't electronics that lined the walls of the tunnel. George's jaw dropped as he panned across the booty with his bright: statues, paintings, sculptures, vases. There were so many old things in here, it was like a museum! George even thought he had seen some of the paintings before. They were famous! He had never been very interested in art, but finding these things down here, in a dark cave . . . they just seemed more interesting, somehow. George had to actually pull himself away to rejoin the others.

"You wouldn't believe it," he explained to the rest of them. "All kinds of valuable stuff is in there. He must have robbed a museum or something!"

Derrick shook his head. "I don't think so. We would have heard about a robbery that big on the news."

"You know, I heard there's a really big black market for stolen art," Shannon said. "If Roulain is smuggling other stolen stuff, why not art? I read somewhere that there are shady art dealers all around the world who will pay for stolen art. Or who will make copies and sell them."

"Something doesn't add up," George pointed out. "If he's got such a large smuggling operation going on down here, then why is he spending so much effort—and money—trying to find a diamond that's only worth about a million dollars?"

"Maybe we should tell someone about this," Renee said, frowning. "Like the cops. If all those things were stolen from museums, they should be sent back."

George hesitated. "You're right, we should tell someone. And we will. But we've got to find the Eye first. We're so close!"

Renee nodded. There would be time to snitch on Roulain's smuggling operation *after* they found the Eye.

With that, they headed back down in the direction of the lake.

The five of them stood at the edge of the underground lake. The dark water spread out before them and disappeared into the darkness beyond. George had thought that the prospect of paddling out onto the lonely waters would be less scary if he was with the whole group. But then a damp current of air blew over him, giving him a chill. It wasn't any less scary. Not one bit.

Paul hung back toward the rear of the group, staying well away from the water's edge. "Paul, we could use someone to stand watch. Since you won't be coming out on the water with us, would you do that?"

Paul straightened up, happy to have a role in the operation. "Okay," he said. "What do I do if I see anyone?"

George thought about it for a moment. It would be too dangerous to have Paul shout something to them. Whoever might be coming would hear it.

Whoooooo!

The ghost wind. Of course!

"Paul, can you make a sound like the ghost wind?"

Paul tried. His first try sounded like a goose being strangled. He and George practiced it together until they both had a sound that was pretty natural. It was close enough to the real ghost wind that it wouldn't arouse suspicion but not so close that they wouldn't be able to tell it apart from the real thing.

"That's it," George instructed Paul. "When we paddle back here, I'll make that sound. If there's anyone nearby or if there's anything else wrong, stay quiet. We'll know to hang back. But if everything is okay, you make the sound back, and we'll know the coast is clear."

"I can do that," Paul said. He started scouting around for hiding places in case someone came.

Renee, Shannon, and Derrick were done inflating the raft. It was time to depart.

"We'll try not to take too long, Paul," Shannon said reassuringly. "We'll be back before you know it!" And with that the four of them shoved off onto the lake.

One thing George hadn't counted on was how much more quickly they were able to travel with four of them in the raft. It helped that the collapsible shovels Renee had brought made excellent paddles. Renee was the best paddler, so she paddled in the rear while Derrick paddled in the front on the other side. Compared to the slow progress George had made paddling with his broken piece of board, this was like being in a speedboat!

They moved so quickly that they made it to the island in no time. They all jumped out of the front of the raft and pulled it up onto the shore of the island so it wouldn't float away.

The island was smaller than it had looked to George when he had seen it from a distance the previous Saturday. He figured it was no more than twenty feet in diameter.

All four of them stayed where they had disembarked from the raft. The back of the tombstone stood before them ominously. None of them seemed eager to be the first to approach it. Shannon finally took the lead and strode bravely around the side.

She looked at the front of it. Her jaw dropped.

"George, I think you'd better take a look at this," she said with an uncertain voice.

Curious, George walked around to the front of the tombstone. Shannon sounded scared. And almost nothing scared Shannon.

He walked up next to her and looked down at the face of the tombstone. It was dull gray stone, and cracks ran through its surface. But the carved letters on its front were still legible. As George read them, he felt like all the air had been pushed out of his lungs.

Here lyes Sergei Trenov.
Wrongly accused
Unjustly killed
1701

Ten

DEAD MAN'S CHEST

Sergei Trenov?

George's mind was swimming. He didn't know what he had expected to find down here, but the name "Trenov" certainly hadn't been it. Could this be the ancestor Kira Trenov had told him about?

"Um . . . George?" Derrick's voice woke George out of his trance.

"Huh?"

"What do you think this means?" Derrick looked as bewildered as George felt. So did Shannon and Renee.

"Do you think your dad's friend is related to . . . the person buried here?" Shannon asked.

"I guess that would make sense . . ." George replied, his mind still racing, trying to piece everything together. "Of course—that would explain why she's been skulking around the tunnels! She told me a story about a Litarian duke. His name was Sergei, and he was sent on a secret mission to retrieve the Eye of Eternity from Captain Kidd.

But he never returned. Everyone thought that Kidd lured him into a trap and killed him."

They all looked like they wanted to avoid George's eyes. Finally, Shannon said what they were all probably thinking. "Well . . . I hate to say it, George, but it looks like that's what happened."

George was usually quick to defend his hero. But now he couldn't think of anything to say. The words on the tombstone mocked him.

Unjustly killed.

Maybe everyone was right after all. Maybe Captain Kidd had been a real pirate. A killer.

George tried to push the thought out of his mind. Whatever the truth was, there was still a treasure to be found. And they weren't going to find it standing around staring at one another.

"We'd better get started," Renee said, breaking the tension. "We don't have all day."

"Are you sure this is the right thing to do?" Derrick asked. "I mean, digging up a dead body? It's one thing when there's a skeleton just lying around in a cave. But actually digging up a grave?"

George thought about it for a moment. "As long as we treat the bones with respect, I think it's okay. If this guy really was murdered, we may actually be doing a good deed. Once we find the treasure, we can make sure the body is buried properly. Aboveground."

"I guess that sounds all right," Derrick said hesitantly. "But I've definitely had my fill of skeletons for a good long time."

They started digging in shifts. Derrick and Shannon dug for a while, but it was harder going than they had thought.

"Why's this dirt so hard?" Derrick groused.

"It hasn't been disturbed in three hundred years," George replied. "It must be pretty hard packed."

"Unfh! If was any harder packed, I'd have two broken arms by now!" Shannon retorted.

After Derrick and Shannon had dug past the point of exhaustion, George and Renee relieved their two friends, who were sweaty and covered with dirt. It didn't take long for George to realize why Derrick and Shannon had been complaining so much. Trying to plant the shovel in the dirt was like trying to dig into concrete. His arms strained and his neck muscles ached as he drove the point of the shovel into the hard ground and then threw a shovelful of dirt over his shoulder.

The hole was getting pretty deep, almost five feet by George's guess. He knew he was four feet, ten inches tall, and the edge was almost over his head. He and Renee were going to need a hand just to get out of the hole!

The dirt was a little different in consistency at this level, George realized. As he thrust his shovel into it, it came loose in large clumps. The clumps of dirt looked moist, almost like clay. *Probably from being surrounded by so much water for so long,* he thought. It made a satisfying wet *schloop* sound when he pulled a shovelful out of the ground. George fell into a rhythmic pattern that helped him keep his mind off how tedious the endless digging was.

Dig. *Schloop!* Toss.

Dig. *Schloop!* Toss.

Dig. *Schloop!* Toss.

Dig. *Tchunk!*

Tchunk?

Tchunk!

"Hey, guys, I've got something!" George shouted excitedly. Renee stopped digging and turned around to look. Derrick and Shannon rushed up to the edge of the hole and peered over. George dropped to his knees and started scooping away dirt from the area his shovel had driven into. Underneath he discovered a smooth, hard surface.

"I think it's wood," George said, digging dirt out of the grooves in the surface. "It feels like it's carved. Renee, help me dig over here."

George and Renee dug around the surface he had uncovered. They were surprised to discover that what was buried under the tombstone wasn't a coffin at all.

"It's too small to be a coffin," George called up to Derrick and Shannon. "No way someone's buried in there, unless they're very, very small." The box was only about eight inches square. George and Renee used the tip ends of the shovels to carefully clear away the sides of the box. They eventually cleared enough dirt for them to try and pull the box free. There was some resistance at first, but it soon came loose with the most satisfying of *shloops*.

George held it in his hands and studied it. It was perfectly square, as deep as it was wide and long. He brushed the moist clay off the sides and saw that it was covered all around with ornate carvings. When cleaned up, it would probably look very nice. And it was probably a pretty valuable historical artifact in its own right.

George handed it up to Shannon and Derrick, who then helped him and Renee out of the hole. They brushed as much of the dirt off their clothes as they could and then resumed puzzling over the box. It was sealed shut, and none of them could manage to get it open. There was a small hole in the front, like a keyhole. But it wasn't like any keyhole any of them had ever seen. It was almost like a diamond shape, with rounded corners. It looked oddly familiar to George, but he couldn't figure out what it reminded him of.

"I don't get it," Shannon said finally. "Where's the body?"

"Huh?" George said, looking up from the keyhole.

"The body. The dead man. You know, whose chest we've got to look in." George could hear a note of frustration in Shannon's voice. And he couldn't blame her. They'd been digging for hours, and when they weren't warmed by the work, the cool drafts of the underground lake chamber chilled them to the bone.

"Yeah, that's right," George replied. "I'm not sure what this has to do with the clue. But it seems like too much of a coincidence for this *not* to be where the map is."

"What was the clue exactly?" Renee asked.

They all looked at Derrick. After all, he had the photographic memory.

"*If ye wish to continue the quest, ye must look deep inside a dead man's chest,*" Derrick recited.

"Hey, wait a minute!" Shannon exclaimed. "That's it!"

"What's it?" George asked, curious.

"It's not a box," she said, rapping her knuckles on the top of it. "It's a *chest*. Get it?"

They all groaned as they realized the play on words. They had been fooled by one of Captain Kidd's clues once again. They had dug the box out of what they had assumed was a grave, so it was quite literally a *dead man's chest*.

"Okay, so the third map is in the chest," Derrick said. "But how are we going to get it open?"

"I'd be just as happy to crack it open with one of these shovels," Shannon said with gusto. "I don't care if it is a valuable antique or heirloom or whatever. I want that map!"

"We can't risk that," George reminded her. "If we start hacking away with shovels, we could destroy the map before Derrick even gets a chance to look at it."

"What fits in that keyhole, do you think?" Renee asked. "It's an awfully funny shape."

"I was thinking that, too," George admitted. "It looks familiar to me somehow, but I can't put my finger on it. If I could just remember where . . ."

George's voice trailed off. He had just caught sight of his watch out of the corner of his eye.

"I didn't realize how long we've been down here. We'd better get back or we'll run smack into my dad while we're still covered head to toe in dirt. And I wouldn't want to have to explain how we got that dirty in the house."

"But what about the chest? The map?" Shannon was still impatient.

"Don't worry about it," George consoled her. "We've got the last map—we just can't get *to* it. But we'll figure out a way, you know we will. We've come too far to let it get away from us."

"Oh, I guess you're right," Shannon admitted. "We're just so close, I want to scream!"

"Save your voice," George advised, "for when we find the Eye!"

George thought they had gone fast when they paddled out to the island. But that was nothing compared to the speed with which they paddled back. Whether it was because they were late or because they were excited to have found the third map, they practically motored back to shore. They were moving so fast, in fact, that George had to slow them down as they approached the shore.

"Quiet," he cautioned. "And stop paddling."

Derrick and Renee lifted their shovels out of the lake. Slowly the sound of water lapping against the sides of the raft subsided as the little rubber boat glided to a stop.

George leaned over the front of the raft and cupped his hands around his mouth. A low, deep sound came forth.

"Whoooooo!"

The sound echoed slightly in the cavernous chamber. Even though the rest of them knew George had made the ghost wind sound, they still shivered.

George waited. Silence.

He looked at the others. They knew what that meant. If Paul didn't respond to George's call with one of his own, Roulain or his men were nearby and it wasn't safe to land the raft. Or something had happened to Paul. George started to regret his decision to let Paul stay behind. A look around at the faces of his friends told him they were thinking the same thing.

"Something must have happened to Paul," George whispered. "We should—"

"Whoooooo!"

They were so surprised to hear the sound, they all almost yelped. But once they realized that everything was all right, they eagerly paddled the raft to the shore. When they landed the raft and hopped ashore, Paul was standing by the water's edge.

"Why did you wait so long to signal back?" George asked. "You almost scared the life out of us!"

"I was checking down the tunnel," Paul replied,

motioning behind him to the tunnel they had used to get to the lake." I thought I heard something, so I went to check it out. But it was just a crawler."

Shannon, who was helping Renee and Derrick deflate the raft, paled at this news.

"So . . . did you find what you were looking for?" George noticed an odd tone to Paul's voice.

"Um, yeah. We did," he responded. "We found the third map. Or at least, we know it's in here." George held up the small chest. "We just have to figure out how to get it out."

"Then I guess you won't come down here anymore. . . ."

George tried to get a look at Paul's face in the dark. Was he actually going to miss them? Paul seemed so tough sometimes that it was hard to know what he was feeling.

George was about to speak, but before he could, Paul said, "You don't belong down here, anyway." And then he was gone, rushing down the tunnel ahead of them.

George was stunned. He wanted to call after him, but he didn't know how far his voice would carry. Roulain and his men might not be in this tunnel, but they might hear him if he started shouting. And George knew there was no way he'd be able to catch up to Paul in the dark tunnels if Paul didn't want to be caught up to.

"What's with him?" Derrick asked.

"I don't know," George answered. "I think he might be mad because he thinks we're not going to ever come down here after we find the treasure."

"But doesn't he know he's our friend? That we'd never just leave him down here?" Shannon asked.

"If only he'd come up to the dayside," Renee said. "I know we could help him. Then we wouldn't have to come down here to see him after we find the Eye."

They didn't have much time to wonder about Paul's motivations, though. They needed to get back to the dayside themselves.

George sat cross-legged on the floor of his room with Captain Kidd's journal in his lap. He was wearing his pajamas, and he had even taken a shower to wash all the dirt off him. In the back-yard he had brushed as much of the mud and clay off his clothes as he could. He hoped his father would think any dirt in the hamper was from the touch football he was supposed to have been play-ing in the park last Saturday.

George wasn't used to having so much time to cover his tracks. He had assumed that once again, he and his friends would get home and have to rush around or make up another story for his father. But his dad and Kira hadn't come home by the time Derrick's mother picked them all up, and George had even had time to get clean.

That was unusual, but it was almost becoming a pattern. It used to be that George's dad was always home exactly when he said he was going to be. But lately something had changed, and now sometimes his dad came home as much as an hour later than he'd said.

Not just something, he thought. *It's her. Kira Trenov.* Ever since she'd started snooping around and spending time with his father, his dad's usual habits had become unpredictable. But why? If anything, George would have thought she would want to spend as much time around their house as possible if she was really sneaking around trying to find out about the treasure hunt.

George shrugged off that thought and tried to get back into the journal. He had hidden it well from his friends, but he had been badly shaken by the discovery of the name on the tombstone. Despite the fact that it had some connection to Kira Trenov, George was upset over what the tombstone seemed to be telling them all. That Captain Kidd had killed Sergei Trenov. That he was every bit the bloodthirsty pirate everyone always thought he was.

Everyone except George, that is. But now even George thought that maybe it was true.

That was why he was reading the journal tonight. He was looking for something, anything. Some clue that implied that things were different from what they all assumed. Something that even hinted Kidd hadn't killed Sergei Trenov in cold blood.

George was disappointed at how . . . ordinary most of the journal was. He had expected page after page of thrilling adventure. Instead he mostly found boring entries about everyday occurrences:

September 9, 1698
Today went to market and purchased 2 chickens and a pig for eating. Also bought some rope and posts for building a fence. Total cost: 37 pence.

Unfortunately, most of the entries were as exciting as that one. Other than the clues they had found, the journal wasn't giving them much useful information. George had volunteered to read the journal through and report back to the others if he found anything interesting. But that hadn't happened yet.

George scanned over several more dry lists of business transactions. His eyelids were getting heavy, and he started to think about going to sleep. Then he found the following passage:

April 23, 1701

Have heard at last from Litaria. They are sending an emissary to retrieve the Eye. I am of mixed feelings about the stone. I intend to return it, yet when I gaze into its crystal depths . . . I wonder if I will be able to part with it. I suppose I cannot know until the moment comes.

The emissary is Duke Sergei Trenov. Have been told he is an honourable man, of decent character. But I must not let my guard down. The one who currently sits on the English throne is no friend to me. Could Litaria intend to improve their standing with the British Crown by handing me over to them at last? No doubt Duke Trenov would consider this a most honourable action in his country's name, no matter what his character.

I must stand wary and be prepared to meet treachery.

George's heart was pounding. He was on to something now! So Kidd had thought that Sergei Trenov might be planning to double-cross him. If that were the case, then it would explain why he had killed the Litarian duke—in self-defense. That was okay. At least it was better than cold-blooded murder.

Just as George turned to the next passage, he

heard the key in the door downstairs. His father and Kira were home. George's first instinct was to climb into bed and pretend to be asleep so he wouldn't have to face Kira Trenov. But then he remembered he had promised his dad he would try to be nice to her. *Even if she is a treasure-hunting spy!*

George reluctantly went downstairs to say hello.

"Well, hi there, George," his dad said happily. "Sorry we're home so late. Time just ran away from us. Did you and your friends have a good time?"

His father stood in the doorway, Kira Trenov standing right next to him. His father held her jacket in his hand. She was wearing a dark blue dress. The familiar necklace hung around her neck.

George's dad looked him in the eye, waiting for a reply. But George didn't say anything.

"George?"

George couldn't say anything if he wanted to. He felt like he couldn't even take a breath, let alone speak. His eyes were riveted on Kira Trenov's neck. He remembered at last where he had seen the strange shape of the keyhole on the lock of the chest.

It was the same shape as the Litarian seal she wore around her neck!

Eleven

RANSOM

"Are you sure?" Shannon sounded skeptical.

George nodded, swallowing a mouthful of the cafeteria's tuna noodle casserole with effort. "It has to be. It's the only thing that makes sense!"

They were at their usual table in the cafeteria the following Monday. Once again George was the odd man out. Everyone else had ordered the Salisbury steak.

"But how could the seal she wears around her neck open the chest? Doesn't that sound like an awfully big coincidence to you? We're hunting for a treasure that's been hidden for over three hundred years, and your dad's professor friend has the key?"

George struggled through another bite of tuna. He kept forgetting that none of them had been around when Professor Trenov had told the story behind her family's seal. "She did say that the seal dated back to the same era. In fact, Sergei Trenov gave it to his wife the same year he disappeared: 1701." George might have also added that that was the same year Captain

Kidd had been hanged as a pirate. But he didn't want to remind them that Captain Kidd might actually have killed Sergei Trenov.

"It may be a coincidence," Derrick said. "But it does make sense. There's only one problem."

"What's that?" Renee asked.

"How do we get the seal off of her long enough to try it on the chest?"

Nobody had an answer for that one.

"It's too bad I told her you already turned in your report on Litaria." George sighed, looking at Shannon. "We could have used that as an excuse."

"Yeah, but even if she wanted to help Shannon on her report, I doubt she'd let the thing out of her sight," Derrick pointed out. "It's a priceless family heirloom."

"And we can't open the chest with her in the room," Renee added. "That would raise more questions than anything."

"Yeah, especially since she's trying to get her hands on the treasure herself!" George said angrily.

"You don't know that for sure," Shannon reminded him. But George didn't want to hear it. He *knew*.

"Hey, I've got an idea," Renee said suddenly.

"What is it?" George was ready to try anything at this point.

"Have you ever heard of gravestone rubbing?" she asked.

Shannon and George had never heard of such a thing, but Derrick was nodding. "We did it on a field trip once. You put a piece of paper on a gravestone and then rub a piece of chalk over the paper. It picks up the letters in the gravestone so you have a kind of copy of it."

"But what does that have to do with the seal?" George asked.

"Simple," Renee went on. "Just tell her you want to make a rubbing of the seal. Say you want a 'historical record' or something. She's a professor— she'll like that."

"But Derrick's right," George pointed out. "She won't want to risk losing it."

"So do it while she's in your house. Just say you want to go upstairs and make a rubbing in your room. She probably wouldn't mind letting it out of her sight if it's staying in the same house."

George thought it over. It might work, he had to admit. And right now "might" was all they had.

"All right," he said. "Let's try it."

"Don't forget," Derrick reminded him. "No looking at the map until we're all there to look at it together!"

*   *   *

George was so excited, he could barely contain himself on the bus ride home. He found himself smiling at all the people who shared the bus with him. Some of them smiled back. George wondered if they could even imagine being as excited as he was right now.

After all the adventures he and his friends had had with this treasure hunt, they were finally about to solve it! Suddenly all the difficulties they'd encountered—the booby traps, the quicksand, even being kidnapped by Roulain—none of them mattered. They were about to find some real treasure. They were going to be rich!

George tried to picture the Eye of Eternity in his mind. He knew it might not be very big—his father had said it could be as small as a pea—but a diamond even that big was worth a lot of money. A million dollars, probably! George couldn't even remember how many zeros that was. Was it nine? Or twelve?

"Earth to George," Derrick said.

George snapped out of it and looked at his friend. "Sorry," he replied. "There's just so much running through my head, it's hard to keep it all straight."

"I know what you mean," Derrick agreed. "Hey, did you ever check up on Kira Trenov's academic credentials at the Oxford University web site?"

"Yeah," George said, sounding a little bit defeated. "Not only is she actually a professor there, but she was voted Professor of the Year last term."

Derrick chuckled. "Maybe she's on the level, George."

"Just because that part of her story checks out doesn't mean she's not up to something," George said a little bit defensively.

Whoops! They were so involved with their conversation, they almost missed their stop. George hurriedly reached up and pressed the black plastic strip on the side of the bus. As the bus pulled up to stop, George and Derrick made their way to the front. "Thanks, mister!" George waved to the driver as he charged off the bus. The driver looked like not many people ever thanked him.

George forced himself to walk, not run, to his house. It wasn't over yet. All he had to do was convince Professor Trenov to let him have the seal for, like, five minutes. But to do that, he'd have to be very cool. He didn't want to give himself away by acting all excited and spazzy. After all, Professor Trenov wasn't to be trusted, whatever Derrick or the students at Oxford University thought. George was sure she was just waiting to seize the Eye for herself. But they were going to show her. She thought she could fool a bunch of kids, but they were going to be the ones putting one over on her!

George suddenly laughed out loud. He had never felt so happy.

But when he entered the house and walked into the living room, something didn't feel quite right. His father sat in his favorite easy chair. But he didn't have a dusty old book open, like usual. Instead he had his head in his hands. As he heard George approach, he looked up. There was a look of shock on his face.

"Oh, George, something terrible has happened!"

George's heart started to pound in his chest. What had happened?

"What . . . what is it, Dad?" George walked up to his dad and put a hand on his shoulder. That was when he noticed his father was holding a crumpled piece of paper in his hand.

"Kira . . . Professor Trenov . . . she's been kidnapped!"

"What?!"

George couldn't believe it. *Kidnapped? But who would . . . ? Why would someone . . . ?*

All of a sudden George had a very bad feeling.

"They say they want a diamond," his father was saying. "But what diamond? I don't have any diamonds! What can they mean?" George's father threw his hands in the air in frustration. The paper he had been holding fluttered to the floor. That was when George noticed that his father was also holding Kira Trenov's seal in his hand. George should have been happy to see that, but somehow it didn't seem so important right now.

George couldn't help himself. He had to know. He picked the paper up off the floor and looked at it. It read:

Dr. van Gelder,
I have Professor Kira Trenov. The seal is proof that I have her. I am not afraid to hurt her. And I will do just that if you do not bring the diamond to me. You know what I mean. I know that you have it or that you will have it soon. If you haven't found it yet, you'd better hurry. You only have until noon tomorrow. At that time I will call and give you instructions on how to bring it to me.
Don't contact the police. I'll know.
—Leroy

George felt like he couldn't breathe.

It's all my fault! he thought. *Every time we thought it was too dangerous, I was the one who talked everyone into continuing. And now look what's happened!*

George saw his father looking up at him. The

painful look on his face made George's whole body tremble with guilt.

"Who's Leroy?" Peter van Gelder muttered. "I don't even know anyone named Leroy!"

George pulled a chair over next to where his dad was sitting. He took a deep breath.

"Dad, there's something I need to tell you."